F
Kom

Kometani, Foumiko

Passover

PASSOVER

PASSOVER

FOUMIKO KOMETANI

TRANSLATED BY THE AUTHOR

Carroll & Graf Publishers, Inc.
New York

Copyright © 1989 by Foumiko Kometani

First Carroll & Graf edition 1989

Carroll & Graf Publishers, Inc.
260 Fifth Avenue
New York, NY 10001

Library of Congress Cataloging-in-Publication Data

Kometani, Fumiko, 1930–
  [Sugikoshi no matsuri.   English]
  Passover / Foumiko [i.e. Fumiko] Kometani.
     p.   cm.
  ISBN: 0-88184-509-4 : $14.95
  I. Title.
PL855.04145S813   1989
895.6′35—dc20   89-30472
                                                                   CIP

Manufactured in the United States of America

Contents

Passover

Observe the month of Abib, and keep the passover unto the Lord thy God: for in the month of Abib the Lord thy God brought thee forth out of Egypt by night.

Thou shalt therefore sacrifice the passover unto the Lord thy God, of the flock and the herd, in the place which the Lord shall choose to place his name there.

Thou shalt eat no leavened bread with it; seven days shalt thou eat unleavened bread therewith, even the bread of affliction; for thou camest forth out of the land of Egypt in haste: that thou mayest remember the day when thou camest forth out of the land of Egypt all the days of thy life. —DEUTERONOMY: 16

The smoothly gliding 747 began its descent just as the movie, a noisy Burt Reynolds farce, ended. The ceiling lights snapped on again and the aisles were suddenly clogged with people, as if a movie in an actual theater were just letting out. My husband looked at the heavy winter overcoat on my lap and frowned. "Why the hell did you bring that? You've had it sitting there on top of you since Los Angeles, cramping us all the way across the country. And it'll only be useless."

It was his fault the coat was on my lap. The

3

passengers in the row in front of us had so much luggage there was no room in the overhead compartment for the coat. And it was Al who had insisted that Jon and I bring only carry-on baggage. He said he just could not stand waiting around at airport baggage carousels and they always lost everything anyway. So Jon and I were not allowed to check anything through; we had to pack our stuff in small tote bags and lug everything on board.

"Anyway," Al shrugged, "we'll soon be in New York." And indeed, the 747 was already well into its descent. It no longer seemed to be effortlessly gliding; now I was aware of the roar of its throbbing engines as it seemed to be circling more than usual in its approach. I lifted the tip of my nose from the soft, warm lining of my coat and placed it against the cold hard windowpane. Outside there was gray smoke swirling. Or was it a thick fog? We seemed to be in the midst of a cloud bank. The plane stopped descending, banked, and started to climb again. I blinked my eyes and continued peering out the window. The fog had thickened; raindrops were sliding down the pane.

We have lived in Los Angeles so long, almost eight years now, that we tend to forget about the rain. Oh, we have our rainy season during the winter, but after that the sky becomes blue; it really clears up, and for the rest of the year we just do not have to concern ourselves about the rain—or rainwear for that matter, like umbrellas and rubbers and boots. In New York, I remembered, the weather did not begin to settle until the end of

Passover

April, when the crocuses, white and yellow and violet, peeked out through the snow; and the forsythia, small lemon-yellow buds on bent boughs, burst forth. The lilacs did not bloom until May, when the trees sprouted their new leaves and the pretty dogwood, white and pink, blossomed; while from the earth itself the tulips and hyacinth bloomed briefly everywhere.

How many years has it been since we have had a vacation? I thought, my nose still pressed against the cold and wet windowpane. I mean, when was the last time the three of us, Al and our fourteen-year-old son, Jon, and I just left the house, locked the door, and went somewhere, anywhere, and stayed there for a whole week? We never could even consider doing it before. And I did not think it was possible that my tiredness, our fatigue, could be cured in just this one week either. But this was exactly what we had been living and waiting for, year after year, with fear and anticipation. And when a friend of ours heard that we were finally going to get away together to New York for an entire week, he arranged for us to borrow his father's two-bedroom apartment in a high-rise on 59th Street, just around the corner from Bloomingdales.

I was overjoyed. We had been taking care of our brain-damaged younger son, Ken, for thirteen years, day and night, and that's not an exaggeration or an over-statement in any way. But then, just recently, we were finally able to place him in a small group residence. And since this was Easter week, with Jon's school on spring break, we three could all enjoy the taste of freedom together. Thirteen years of sleepless nights and dirty dinner tables and messy toilet accidents and violent temper tantrums were suddenly over. After Ken left our house and entered the group residence something seemed to leave my body, too. A sense of utter fatigue suddenly lifted from my legs and waist, and a charge of new energy, as if spring itself were breaking out inside me, surged through me. Sometimes I would stop for a moment and feel guilty, blame myself for being such an uncaring mother. But the closer the plane came to New York the less I did so and the more my spirits soared.

What would I do in New York? For fourteen years, first with Jon and then always with Ken, I had a baby in my house demanding my complete attention and concentration, never giving me a single moment to myself or a solitary chance to really think about myself. I wanted first to see my friend Alice. I had not seen her for eight years. How old was she now? Thirty-five? And she was probably still working as a dental hygienist. Alice had the classical features of the Buddha in Gandala: a very wide forehead that proclaimed her wisdom, and beneath it, wonderfully clear hazel eyes. When I phoned her, I knew she would sigh and then scream in delight, "Michi, where are you?"

Alice and I first met at a parents' meeting of Jon's nursery school. At that time I rarely ran across another Asian, let alone a Japanese, so whenever I saw any Asian at all I felt both sympathetic and nostalgic. "You come from India?" I asked her immediately. She was not at all surprised by my

question. "Everyone asks me that," she replied
politely, "but I'm more American than anyone else
here. I have white blood and black blood and American Indian blood all mixed up inside of me. And if
you ever met my parents and brothers and sister
you'd really see how many kinds of different races
are living in me." And then she smiled at me
warmly even though I was still a stranger to
her.

"If you wore a sari and put a red dot between
your eyebrows," I still insisted, "you would look
completely Indian."

"Yuh, I know," she nodded, staring at me with
those big hazel eyes, another warm smile forming
on her amber-colored face. "Meanwhile, I'm black."

I did not realize then that Alice was Steve's
mother. Jon was three years old, and Steve was
the first friend he made at nursery school. When he
came home from school he was always talking
about Steve. Until I met Alice that evening I never
guessed that Steve was a kid of mixed races just
like Jon, and somehow it surprised me.

In New York I would certainly look up Elaine
again, too. We first became friends sixteen long
years ago, in Japan. Elaine had piercing black eyes
and bound up her black hair in a chignon like a
ballerina. I remember when we would drive in her
car to the Co-op Market near the Ashiya Station,
the bourgeois Japanese women would all look at
her and laugh, pointing at her skirt, and I would
feel embarrassed. The Japanese women would be
laughing at the patchwork design of Elaine's
skirt, assuming in their ignorant fashion—or igno-

rance of fashion—it was faulty, slapdash mending. The memories of the wartime days, when they all had to wear mended clothing, of course, were still too real for them to realize that such a style could possibly represent the latest in fashion. I last spoke with Elaine when she called to tell me her husband had left her. "But do not worry," she said. "My son and I will manage. At least we still have the apartment."

When we were still living in Westchester County, I would sometimes meet Elaine in Manhattan for lunch. And whenever I complained about the prejudice I was always running into in America, Elaine would tell me about the problems of her own mother, who was French and spoke English with a thick accent. Even as a child, Elaine remembered how salespeople in department stores, for example, were always mimicking her mother's speech behind her back.

So soon I would be seeing both Alice and Elaine again. We would lunch together, go to a museum, and we would talk. There were so many things to talk about. I felt the keen pleasure of anticipation as I looked out the window. It was raining harder now, huge raindrops hitting the window, splattering, and then sliding down the pane like tears flowing down a child's cheeks.

The FASTEN YOUR SEAT BELT sign flashed on. And then the flat voice of the Captain came over the PA system:

"We might be a little late tonight, folks. About thirty minutes or so. Because JFK is really jammed, and we'll just have to wait our turn to get in there.

Sorry about that. And because of the storm, we might encounter some air turbulence at this altitude. So please keep your seat belt fastened and just wait it out with us. Thank you."

Almost immediately the plane rocked from side to side and dipped suddenly, like a cable car going down a mountain slope in measured stops, and then, as if it had reached the last stop, abruptly it began to circle back up again. Clouds of white smoke were rising everywhere outside the window to the left when a wavy gray shape appeared through a golden haze; and to the right of the 747's gray body, behind the rain clouds, a beautiful rainbow formed in a semicircle. At one moment it was like a drawing in a children's book of two huge angels with large white wings on their backs; the next moment it seemed the traditional Japanese illustration of thunder bearing drums. For a split second the world around me was like a rapidly changing children's picture book.

In reality, what had happened was this: Another plane, silvery and shining, had approached us from below, while our plane was falling then rising in counter-clockwise circles. And no sooner was my body adjusted to turning left than the plane was climbing to the right again. Al, who had been constantly talking to Jon, was unusually quiet. His square sun-burnt face seemed to have lost its Los Angeles glow, and he was staring straight ahead without focusing. He leaned forward, and his slender fingers rifled through the flight magazine and the dinner menu and the life saving instructions in the pouch on the back of the seat before him until

9

he picked out a white paper sack. And then, despite the Captain's announcement and the fact that the FASTEN YOUR SEAT BELT sign was still on, he rose and rushed up the aisle without saying a word.

As I listened to the sounds of the rain, tossed by the gusty winds against my window, the airplane's public-address system clicked on again. This time it was not the captain but the Chief Flight Attendant, asking in a voice of unnaturally forced calm if there was a doctor on board, preferably a cardiologist. When I heard that, the bottom seemed to drop out of my stomach. Was something the matter with Al? He did have heart disease; his right coronary artery was completely blocked. But he had medication for that. And he always carried his nitroglycerine pills in case of sudden angina. I was certain he had some in his pocket. Could his heart have been affected by the plane's yo-yoing up and down in a circular holding pattern?

The public-address system came on again. "This is to remind you that the FASTEN YOUR SEAT BELT sign is still on. Will all passengers remain in their seats, please."

I began to worry. Perhaps the flying conditions had really become bad. And how long had it been since Al had left his seat? I looked up and down the aisle. The passengers in the row behind us had been talking and laughing in loud voices throughout the trip. But now they were not laughing. They were not even talking anymore. Instead, all I could hear was the sound of hail pellets bouncing against the window. I peered out and saw the same airplane I had seen before. Perhaps it was waiting to get into JFK, too. Our plane rattled for a second and squeaked loudly as either hail or rain, I could not tell which now, continued to bombard the windowpane. And suddenly I sensed something going wrong with the vacation. Even the cloud movements seemed to have become strange and ugly.

If the plane were to crash it would not matter very much whether Al was sitting next to me or not, or whether I had my coat on my lap, for that matter. Dead was dead, naked or wearing your best suit, hungry or after having eaten a most delicious meal, even though after we were dead our friends might wonder if we had been sitting next to each other, holding hands as the plane went down. They could not possibly imagine that Al was in the aluminum toilet vomiting as the 747 hit the ground. But if this plane were to crash I would feel terribly cheated; I had so looked forward to this vacation's draining my body of its fatigue. I was tired to the death, but I did not want to be tired at my death. Somehow that would be the hardest death of all to accept, I decided, and I refused to resign myself to that fate.

Jon removed the earphones, which had been fixed to his ears since takeoff. His usually shining black eyes had clouded over. "What's Daddy doing?" he asked.

I shrugged as the hail continued to hit the window, one, two, three small white pellets piling up on the window ledge and then disappearing, and the plane rocked from side to side. For a brief moment I felt the airplane food slowly trying to rise up from my stomach, and my spirits immediately began to fall. But then it was over. Perhaps Al was suffering from motion sickness? Before we left the house I took two Sankyo pills to aid digestion and ward off nausea. I always did that, even if we were just going for a short car ride. That was my habit. And Al and Jon, as usual, teased me about it. "Sankyo for this. Sankyo for that. Sankyo for everything," they said. But it was working. Fortunately, I was not feeling that bad. Maybe Al should have taken Sankyo, too. Or, at least, not teased me about it. Perhaps that was why he was being punished.

The plane was descending again when I saw Al coming down the aisle. I was relieved. At least the cardiologist had not been for him. I sat back in my seat and waited for him to rejoin me. But it took him a long time. Whenever the plane pitched or jerked he had to stop and hold on to the backs of the seats on both sides of the aisle. Finally, he sat down beside me, saying, "I vomited." Then he sighed. "And now I feel better."

His complexion, indeed, did have its color back, and his round brown eyes had their luster and twinkle again. But his thin chestnut hair, which he had taken to stretching like silk fiber across the top of his forehead, smoothing it down with both hands, still looked to me like a comic attempt to conceal his ever increasing baldness. I laughed as he leaned back and buckled his seat belt, and then I breathed in deeply, clasping my overcoat with both hands.

*   *   *

Passover

Some of our fellow passengers shouted joyously, others expressed their relief in applause when the plane finally landed, an hour late. But my own relief ended when we stepped out of JFK into the dusk of an icy rain that pierced my cheeks with pain. The dark branches of the trees around the airport, like some sort of fragile wirework sculpture, appeared to shake in the mist of the smoky gray rain. And the lawns they stood on, still the gray-white of winter, surprised me. What a difference from Los Angeles, where the tall palm trees rose in stately columns, bright red-and-white flowers blooming everywhere around them. New Yorkers might somehow find a hint of spring in this weather, but to me, accustomed to Southern California, it was colder than the dead of winter.

I was shocked that I had so easily forgotten so much. After all, I did live here for eight years and had learned to take the severe climate as a matter of course. And somehow I did remember enough to be wearing an overcoat with a hood that covered my head. But Jon had only a thin windbreaker over a sweater and Al an unlined raincoat. As we waited for a taxi I cast a quick glance at my shivering husband and shrugged my shoulders under my warm overcoat. *See, big mouth.*

The primary reason we had moved to Los Angeles from New York was the extremely cold winters. I grew up in the Kansai region of Japan where the winter is mild. I could not bear the wet cold of a New York winter and thought I would never forget it. But evidently I had. And once I stepped out of the airport terminal that fact shocked me even more than the sting of the cold itself. I hated

13

to think that I might have become like the men in both Japan and America alike, always acting indifferently about weather and temperatures, as if such concerns were beneath one's dignity—or masculinity. But the truth of the matter is, the real reason I brought an overcoat along had nothing to do with a conscious awareness of the extreme temperature differential I would be facing.

The winter before we moved to Los Angeles, I bought a well-made but expensive fleece-lined ski coat at a sportswear shop on Fifth Avenue whose name I could never pronounce—Abercombrie & Fitch. My husband would always laugh whenever I tried to say that name. He would also tease me because I never had the occasion to wear the coat in Southern California. Not even once. So this time, I thought, at last I have the opportunity, and I pulled it out from the back of the closet.

The three of us got into a taxi so old and battered I feared it would break down before we reached our destination in Manhattan and could breathe in the tough air of the city itself. Night had fallen, red and yellow-blue neon lights refracted through the rain in a colorful mist that reflected against the pitch black, blinking sky. Large American-built cars filled the width of each lane of a parkway that had fewer lanes than a Los Angeles freeway. When we crossed the Queensborough Bridge, the tall, darkened buildings of Manhattan rose up ominously before us. The taxi's headlights shone into streams of rain that seemed to become white threads dancing on a loom. In

Los Angeles everything is flat, two dimensional, like a street map. I need never look up; the sky always spreads out before me. But here in New York the sky was suddenly directly overhead, I would have to bend my neck back to perceive it, boulevards in the air cutting between the high rises. Even after living in America for twenty years, it still came as a suprise to me that a single nation could have two cities so completely disparate as New York and Los Angeles. Except for its two months of rain, Los Angeles is forever dazzling and endlessly bright. New York is more congenial to moods of quiet, but you also feel the imminent threat of depression in the weaker light of the North. If there were suddenly no more airplanes and everyone had to depend on the archaic American railroads, I think in a hundred years these two great cities, a continent apart, would evolve into races and societies of completely different people, utterly unable to communicate with each other.

The apartment we were borrowing was in a white brick East Side high-rise building on 59th Street off Third Avenue, with an impressively large lobby bathed in the light of a giant chandelier. The doorman, in a dark brown paramilitary uniform, had asked our identity and then repeatedly checked it against the letter of permission the owner of the apartment had left behind. Finally satisfied, he opened the drawer of a tall desklike rostrum and leafed through a bunch of envelopes, like a post-office worker sorting mail, until he found the one he was looking for. From it he extracted a set of keys and daintily handed them to us, as if they were the keys to the city itself. Given New York's reputation for crime, I wondered if it was all part of some quaint prayer ritual for safety.

The door to the apartment itself had two upper keyholes and one lower one, and after Al discovered through trial and error which key fit which, he was able to push it open. Immediately we were assailed by the acrid smell of the cleaning liquid, Pine-Sol. Since the owner of the apartment wintered in Florida, nobody had lived there for months. But the heat was turned on full blast, and the dry air seemed to rip the moisture off my rain-soaked skin. Why on earth, I wondered, do they have to heat this apartment during this period of great oil shortage?

Al flicked the switch on the foyer wall and the light came on. I took off my overcoat and hung it in the hall closet. Meanwhile, Jon and Al, having dropped our bags in the middle of the foyer, were opening bathroom and bedroom doors and turning on lights everywhere.

A small kitchen opened off the right side of the foyer, and to the left of it was a living room with a dining alcove. At each end of the apartment was a bedroom with a bathroom of its own. It was a very functional layout. I liked the large living room because it was sparsely furnished. On a red lacquered Oriental chest were painted Chinese figures and landscapes. A black rosewood table stood neatly and serenely before a golden sofa, and a few handsome red-brocaded wood-framed chairs lined the walls. Usually Americans and Europeans crowd too much furniture and too many decorations into too little space. But this room had no clutter. It calmed me down.

I crossed the living room and went to the window, anxious to rid the room of the Pine-Sol odor. I like the scent of fresh pine, but this strong chemical smell could soon give me a headache. I parted the white satin curtains and pulled up on the square iron handles with both hands. But the heavy window would not move. The panes were thick, and the sash had been painted over often. With great effort I finally did manage to raise the window a few inches.

The concrete ledge outside was wet. Suddenly, as if having climbed up the precipice of bare wall for precisely twenty two stories and having been aimed directly at the window opening, which was less than the width of my own hand, the traffic sounds below leaped into the room. I felt as if I were standing atop a factory. Brakes abruptly applied, automobiles slipping and skidding on the wet streets, drivers angrily honking their horns at each other and honking hysterically at the pedestrians who were blithely ignoring the traffic signals, I could hear it all, over two hundred fifty feet below. The street, made shiny by the rain, glistened like a black vinyl tape on which were toy model cars that rarely moved, not even when the signals changed to green. And then the gasoline smell, too, assailing me, reached the window. After all the difficulty I had had in opening it, I quickly closed the window. I did not want to let that much of the big city in at once.

On the rain-washed tile wall of the building across the street the reflections of neon lights flickered in pink and yellowish mauves. It was a tall building, at least thirty stories high, but not a single light burned within it, making its many windows look like small dark shrines. In a smaller building next door, lined up in a single horizontal line like rows of cards in a game of solitaire, were boxes of rectangular light. I wondered who could possibly be working at this late hour. Probably a Japanese trading company, I decided. Beside that bulding a cluster of old, four-storied brownstones stood. The ground floor of one of the brownstones had a shop with a sign above its entrance, but I could not make out what it said. Behind the brownstones stacks of taller buildings rose like children's construction blocks. I could see the bare branches of dead trees and the silhouette of a patio umbrella on the rooftop of one of them. Could that be a penthouse garden?

As I looked down at the street I remembered the first time I arrived in New York, twenty years ago, after a two-week-long freighter trip from Japan to San Francisco and then a long rail trip across the country. When I stepped onto the streets of Manhattan I saw steam seeping out of manholes, like the vapor rising from hot springs in Japan. I nervously swallowed my acid spittle, wondering what could possibly be going on beneath those thick beds of concrete and asphalt. And I did not spot a single Japanese person whom I might ask. Back in 1960 there were few Japanese people in New York. In fact, there were but two Japanese restaurants in the entire city, one up near Columbia and the other, the Miyako, in midtown.

Since I am quite petite in size, I had to arch myself backwards to look upward and see the tops of the tall buildings. Like a country tourist, I would walk down Madison Avenue or up Fifth Avenue that way. Often busy New Yorkers bumped into me. But I soon learned to be careful and avoided getting knocked into the gutter.

I had sailed under the Golden Gate Bridge in San Francisco, and now I wanted to climb to the top of the Empire State Building. Manhattan was not as dirty then as it is now, but it still teemed with garbage, paper, and vinyl bits blown about in the wind, and I remember being surprised at the amount of trash that was piled at the foot of that great building.

I took a Circle Line tour boat around Manhattan and saw the international, modern box-style United Nations Buildings complex along the river and the classically graceful Brooklyn Bridge. I was constantly astonished by the grandness of the architectural scale; there was nothing I could compare it to in Japan at the time. I visited the one-man shows of painters whose work I was familiar with from art-book reproductions and art-magazine illustrations, and I fervently dreamed that one day I would have one-man—or rather one-woman—shows of my own in similar galleries. There was freedom in America. I could do whatever I wanted to do. I had finally made the great leap out of Japan, where convention reigned and all men had much more power than any woman. I could live the romantic life of my dreams, one dedicated purely to art and its values.

Just after the war, in the new American Pharmacy on Toa Road in Kobe, I smelled a fragrance, one that I had never smelled before. It did not come from any one item, but was everywhere in the store. I decided that must be the aroma of America, and it became the symbol of freedom for me. Now I could sniff the ambience of the American Pharmacy everywhere.

Twenty years had passed since then. Now I had to call Elaine and Alice and set up a museum schedule. I particularly wanted to go to the Frick. I was sure Jon would enjoy seeing the kind of mansion rich people once lived in, the marbled floors, the fountain in the atrium. And, of course, the splendid yellows in the Turners hanging there. I wanted him to see those paintings. I also wanted to shop at Saks for new shoes. . . .

"Hello, Sylvia. How are you?"

The sound of Al's loud voice on the phone in the kitchen immediately drained away all the pleasure I had been anticipating. He could have at least waited until tomorrow before calling her. I left the window and went into the kitchen.

Al was wearing a green woolen sweater over brown-and-white hound's tooth checked slacks, a crumpled tissue dangling from a pocket. My sister-in-law Sylvia was four years older than Al, but she once asked us to say that she was three years younger than Al. Anyone seeing them together could have told at once that simply was not so. Besides all of Al's friends in New York knew he had an older sister. And I did not have anyone to tell that lie to. I had never met any of her office colleagues, nor did I intend to. And I did not have any Japanese friends in New York anymore. Even if I had, they could not have cared less whether Sylvia was forty-nine or fifty-six. Why should they?

Sylvia was one of the reasons we moved to Los Angeles from New York. Her living in New York had made the whole city seem very depressing to me, because she was always quick to apply her specially developed skills to make even those who had nothing to do with her feel guilty. For example, once we left our cat with her over the weekend. When I went on Monday to her apartment to pick it up she said to me sharply, "The cat is finally getting used to me and you are going to take her away, too." She simply did not care a whit—or give a shit—about my feelings.

She was the sort of person, you see, who could talk on and on over the phone, an hour at a time, screwing up my day completely, not letting me get my housework done, even when I was trying to feed two babies. Even when I said Ken had soiled his pants and I had better change him quickly, she still would not listen to me. She did not care to hear my troubles. "My boss made an ironical comment recently," she said. "And I am afraid I might be fired. So I have to start thinking about looking for another job. That is why I am so depressed. And I'm so lonely, too. Living alone, you know, I have nobody to talk to and there is nobody to listen to me." And she went on talking continuously about herself and her agony. I had to listen carefully for a chance to interrupt and hang up. But then if she sensed I was listening, she took advantage. "For my vacation," she proudly continued, "I went to Sweden." *A vacation anywhere would be pie in the sky to me.* "The nights were white, you know. I couldn't sleep. I became so tired. But I did buy a baby seal overcoat. I'll show it to you the next time I visit."

If you bring that coat I will be so nervous. I can just see Ken smearing ice cream and rice and mashed potatoes all over it. Don't you realize what would happen? Anyway, how dare you wear such a coat? A baby animal had to be killed so it could be made. How insensitive can you be? What kind of nerve do you have?

"I asked my super to take care of my cats while I was gone. When I came back I found they had become so skinny, and there was no luster to their hair. Maybe I should give them wheat germ. What do you think? Or should I bring them to the vet first?"

Who cares? I had to restrain myself from shouting, because if I did, then I would have to answer three or four more hysterical telephone calls. So I swallowed the words and my stomach turned sour. Meanwhile Ken had taken the feces out of his underpants and begun to smear it all over the bathroom. And it was too late for me to stop him.

What a rotten sister-in-law! If we moved to California, a long distance phone call would cost her seventy-nine cents for the first minute and fifty cents for every minute after that. So she certainly would not talk more than thirty minutes. It was something to consider. Or maybe she should move to California? Without her around, New York could be a cheerful place to live.

"If we happened to run into Sylvia on the street,"

my husband turned to me, his hand covering the mouthpiece, "we would have no excuse." Which was an excuse in itself, proving he was afraid of Sylvia. Fifty-two years old and still afraid of his sister. I just could not understand this American woman and that American man.

"Uncle Irving is coming?" Al was speaking into the phone again. "Yes, I would like to see him. I have not seen him for twenty years. . . . When is it? . . . Oh, I will be there. I definitely will be there." He was making a commitment without even consulting me. And I was sure it involved his sister. Wherever he said he was going, Sylvia was sure to be there, too.

"I'll call you back. I have to tell Michi and Jon. They might have their own plans. . . . Okay. What? The subway goes on strike tomorrow? I didn't know that. Then we can't go anywhere. We can only go as far as we can walk for sure. . . . Where is Ellen's apartment? . . . Can I get a cab there? With a strike it'll be murderous. . . . I'll call you back. . . . Okay . . . Good night." As he put down the receiver my husband looked at me awkwardly. "Michi, Passover starts thiis week," he said. "I'd forgotten completely. And Sylvia says my cousin Ellen can invite us to their Seder."

"Which day is that?"

A long time ago, before our children were born, I attended a Passover Seder at Al's aunt's house, and it was not such a wonderful experience for me. That aunt's family was not particularly religious and did not make such a big thing out of Passover. My clearest remembrance is of eating a gigantic matzoh ball. It was floating in a bowl of chicken soup. Or, rather, the other way around: more like the chicken soup was sprinkled over the matzoh ball.

"Monday night is the first Seder. Passover and Easter come at the same time this year."

I was not surprised that the festivals of spring, whether Jewish, Catholic, or Protestant—or even Buddhist for that matter, such as Higan—all came at the same time. Spring is spring. Still I did not like the idea of our being in New York during Passover. It was Saturday night, and if we said the three of us could come on Monday night, that was really short notice for the hostess. We probably would not wind up going there anyway. So I decided to try to make light of the whole matter.

"How does Sylvia know your cousin Ellen can prepare enough matzoh balls to have three more for dinner Monday night? That's real *chuzpa*."

"Sylvia said she will talk to Ellen. But there is always room for more at a Seder, it's part of the ancient tradition. Anyway, according to Sylvia, Ellen is only too glad to have us, because her father, my old Uncle Irving, is very anxious to see me. And there'll be a lot of good food to eat—besides matzoh balls. You can relax and just eat and drink. Let's go."

If they could easily add any number of people to the Seder, it seemed there was no way out of it for me. Their tradition was my problem, because I did not want to go. I hate all religion. And now I would have to see Sylvia twice. Because I was sure we would also have to take her to lunch or dinner.

I did not know if I could take seeing Sylvia twice in one week.

"You know another cousin of mine, Marilyn," Al was saying, "is going to have a Seder the following night, Tuesday. And Sylvia suggested we could go there, too. She can ask Marilyn."

So Sylvia was really trying to regain her tight hold on her brother. A chill ran through me from the top of my neck all the way down my backbone. In Los Angeles I had many Jewish friends. I did not become friends with these people because my husband was Jewish. We just became friends naturally. But I did wish to be excused from meeting certain Jewish women. Of course there was Sylvia. But there were also other women in his family, his cousins and his aunts. They never made me feel they recognized our marriage. One reason may have been that I did not convert to Judaism. But I also always wondered if perhaps it was because I was not white. None of these women attended the wedding party Al's friends gave for us in a Park Avenue apartment, where I walked on shaking heels across a slippery marble floor. And we never received any gifts from them either.

Why on earth did Sylvia think we had come to New York? To see her and Al's cousins? I did not know what kind of people these cousins were, but if they were Sylvia's age and had Sylvia's personality, I knew there was no way I could take a double Sylvia for two nights. That would be too much. I did not come to New York to torture myself and I would not allow Sylvia to destroy my long deferred pleasures. After all these years I was going to enjoy my one week of freedom.

"I have just a single week for vacation," I raised my voice angrily. "And it would be absurd for me to spend two nights like that."

"Me too," screamed Jon like a crane in heat. "I don't like religious crap." He had been leaning against the wall between the kitchen and the living room, listening to us, his straight black Japanese hair falling down over his face and almost covering the bridge of his nose. It was hard to tell whether the nose would suddenly grow large like a Jewish nose or fall away and become a small, stubby Japanese nose. "I came to New York to meet friends. I want to see Peter and Stevie. And, Daddy, you promised to take me to see some plays on Broadway, too!"

When Al saw the two of us were not about to give in so easily, he thrust out his square jaw and tried another approach. "Passover is more than just a religious holiday. It is a celebration of freedom for the Israeli slaves who were emancipated from the Egyptian Pharaoh three thousand years ago. And it is also a festival of spring, happy and joyous." *Happy and joyous, with Sylvia there?* But although I was in the same position as Jon, reluctant to have anything to do with religion, a curious impulse to observe Uncle Irving and his daughter's family came over me. Out of Al's dozens and dozens of cousins, I knew only two. Ben, who was a famous pop singer, and Bernie, who was notoriously frugal. I wondered if the others could really be as mean as Al's sister, or if there might not be some normal human beings among them. I began to rationalize that I might even learn a thing or two.

But just the mention of religion has always been enough to induce a yawn in me. It used to bore me stiff having to listen to the Buddhist priest's prayer, *"Namu ami dabutsu."* But at least the Buddhist priests never cared whether you believed in their prayer or not. In the home of my parents, whenever the Buddhist priest came to pray at the family altar, it was my Christian mother who had to greet him and assist him in the ritual. No one else would assume that task. And what perhaps annoyed me the most after I came to live in America were the Christian missionaries who were trying to convert non-Christians such as myself. No matter how many times I said, "No!" they would still return, importunate as spring flies. Many Japanese may have converted to Christianity not because of a spiritual quest culminating in a pure belief but rather as the result of sheer physical exhaustion. Judaism does not apply the pressure of missionaries the way Christianity does, but they still seem to insist that their own God is Almighty and imply that any other religion is basically heretical. In Buddhism there are no set times for communal prayer services at the temples except for memorial ceremonies. However, in Western religions you are expected to go to the church or the synagogue to worship God in daily and weekly scheduled services. Whenever I attended such services, I would feel the other worshippers had gathered to bring pressure upon me. After spending years together in a tightly knit group, they all seemed to speak in the same jargon and move with the same gestures, making me feel completely isolated and alienated. They were like children and adolescents who herd in their own closed circles, conforming to the group, shunning any individualistic expression. Al recognized that fact, too, and when we married we promised each other that we would avoid all the unpleasantness the difference of religions could cause, by not insisting on the religions of either of our families. We were not cultural representatives; there was no need to wave our religious banners—or flaunt our backgrounds. Besides, neither of us was religious in the first place.

And that was the way we got along for twenty years. But from the beginning of our marriage it was Al who had the problem keeping that promise. I was not a believer, but I had read the Bible and Buddhist books out of a native curiosity. No one in my family ever tried to lead me toward religion, let alone drum religion into my head. But Al had been brought up in a family that believed in Judaism, the origin and foundation of all Western religion. At the age of eight days, he underwent the religious rite of circumcision. His family further laid out clear, strong religious lines for him to follow as a growing child. He attended synagogue with his parents on holidays and studied Hebrew at a special school, so that at the age of thirteen he could go through the Bar Mitzvah ceremony.

While we were living in New York, Al was always making excuses to Sylvia whenever Jewish holidays came along. But after we moved to Los Angeles there was no need for him to do so. And gradually, without any relatives around to remind us of the holidays, we both became indifferent to their occurrence. So when my husband said, "Let us attend the Passover Seder," I flinched. Had he lost his mind? Had he suddenly become old and sentimental? And if he was this way now, what would happen when he reached seventy? Would he be trotting off to the synagogue every Friday night and Saturday morning? Al's father's family was strictly Orthodox, a long line of rabbis, generation after generation. What if he were to finally become a rabbi, too? I felt more vexed than amused. I would have no choice but to divorce him in a minute. I did not want to waste an unnecessary second on something as nonsensical as religion. I saw nothing redeeming about any expertise regarding any ancient but illogical body of irrational beliefs and practices. What good were they? What value was there in them? At best, religion led to serious lip service and hypocritical actions. If you wanted to act with virtue, I firmly believed, it was not necessary to thread your way through the ancient tangles of religion. The first people to speak out against nuclear arms were not Christian pastors or Buddhist monks. Religion has always looked to death, even admired death. The people who first opposed nuclear weaponry, Linus Pauling, Bertrand Russell, and Jean-Paul Sartre, did not belong to any organized religion. In our present era, the ultimate virtue is an affirmative attitude toward life, not death.

29

The Passover Seder involved traditional ritual and ceremony. Attending without knowing the ritual or the ceremony, one would appear a fool. There was no room to make mistakes. And on the contrary, any fool who knew the ceremony could appear wise as he proudly showed off his knowledgeability. That sort of thing always irritated me. I never wanted any part of it, which was why I had never fostered religious beliefs of any sort on Jon.

Al's temples twitched as I reminded him of my convictions. And our joint opposition, Jon's and mine, seemed to overwhelm him. "Okay, look," he said quickly, holding up his hands. "I will accept an invitation to only one Seder." He acted as if he was trying to please us. I knew he was afraid we would still refuse to attend any Seder.

"When we lived in Japan," I reminded him, "I never asked you, nor did you ever have to, go to any Buddhist ceremony. And that involved a period of over two years. This is just a one-week vacation, and it is as if I asked you to attend some Buddhist ceremony twice. Can't you see that? Besides, have you no memory? The relatives we'll see there were against our marriage. Your damned relatives! They were not at our wedding celebration, either. But as your name became a little well known, suddenly they discovered how close they were to you. But we are not for public view. I remember meeting one of your aunts just after we were married. She inspected every inch of me as she looked me over from the top of my head down to the tips of my toes. I felt like my skin was burning under a scorching summer sun. Were there horns sprouting out of my head? Were there wings growing on my feet? Did I have the ears of a donkey? She investigated my face as if she was really concerned that I might have some breathing difficulties. After all, my nose was so small and flat compared to hers. Maybe she thought I did not have two nostrils?" I shook my head vigorously. "I do not want to go through that sort of thing again."

"You won't have to. But I do want to see Uncle Irving again. He's eighty-three, and I know you'd like him."

I laughed. "When we first met you talked that way about Sylvia. I imagined your sister was like some movie actress, a Claire Bloom or a Lauren Bacall. Then I met her and I wanted to run away at first sight. I thought you must be blind, or really have a creative imagination. I am not talking simply about the fact that she did not have a pretty face. You do not have to have a pretty face for the heart to show on it. But Sylvia had such a mean face. In Japan there is an old saying: 'One sister-in-law is worth a thousand goblins.' But that was the domestic rate of exchange only, applying only to Japan. Sylvia was so big and fat she equaled ten thousand goblins. And if you considered her total body power, probably even more. So I cannot depend on your words, as far as your family is concerned."

"Look, I'll only go to Ellen's. So please come with me," Al said. His hands were pressed together as if in supplication, making it seem no matter how opposed I was to the idea of going to any Passover Seder, I had no choice but to compromise.

"Okay," I shrugged. "Only Ellen's." But the moment I said that, I felt caught in a well-laid trap.

"No way! There is no way I'm going!" shouted Jon in a dry, stricken voice that seemed stuck to the mucous membranes of his throat. "I'll stay here myself and I'll eat dinner alone. You and Mom can go by yourselves." His body twisted and turned as if racked with pain, and there were tears in his big black eyes.

Once I had decided to go, I thought it would be a good idea for Jon to come, too. Even unwillingly. Meeting his relatives—or so-called relatives—could prove worthwhile. After all, neither Al nor I had any relatives in Los Angles; my parents and brothers and sister were all in Japan; and if Jon were to grow up without knowing anyone else in our families existed, what would happen after we died? Left alone with just his brain-damaged brother on this vast and endless continent, he would feel terribly lonely and isolated. I always worried about that. Even if he was a unique amalgam of different genes, each element that went into that composition, one by one, could be found scattered among his relatives.

I tried explaining all that to him. "Jon, it is not a bad idea to know the faces of your relatives in New York. You have no other uncles or aunts or cousins in America. And you never know when you might have to call upon them in an emergency. And Aunt Sylvia, you know, is single, and does not have any children of her own, either. It is just one night. Go look at everybody's face." At bottom, of course, I was trying to convince myself, as much as to persuade him.

"I don't like religion," Jon said, biting his lower lip and looking down in a pout. Then he pushed back his thick black hair and rubbed his eyes.

I put my hand on his shoulders sympathetically. "Neither do I," I said.

There were only two days until the Passover Seder. I hoped by then Jon's brain cells would compute the right decision. I never wanted to be accused of trying to force any form of religion upon him. But I also did not want him to spend an evening alone, far from home.

Snow. Snow. Snow. Even though it was April, it was coming down in droves. Fiftieth floor. Thirtieth floor. Twentieth floor. Some times the snow fell in masses of white powder, at other times in individual flakes that scattered, whirling about. It was as if people were throwing soybeans during the Setsubun Festival from the tops of skyscrapers. We cursed the snow. It was nearly seven o'clock, and for three-quarters of an hour we had been trying to catch a taxi.

The hoards of people scurrying home across the sidewalks, lit by the yellow rays of phosphorescent streetlamps, quickly converted the fallen snow into a gray slush. By comparison, the sidewalks in Los Angeles were always clean and empty, except for the few people hopping across them like jumping beans, anxious to get out of the sun and back into their cars. And the New Yorkers, I noticed, except for Asians and blacks, all seemed pale. In addition, most of them walked as if they were being forced to carry heavy, weighted objects, large in volume, about their waists. Perhaps everything was exaggerated because of the subway and bus strikes, but there was no way we could take two steps without someone bumping into us.

I shivered in this unaccustomed weather. Fortunately, I had my overcoat to shiver into. Al and Jon, wearing only a thin raincoat and a windbreaker, could only shake their legs and shrink their shoulders. But I had warned them. Now they could have big goose bumps to go along with their big mouths.

Yellow taxi after yellow taxi passed us by. When one did stop, somehow a shrewd New Yorker would appear, to beat us into it. By the time we finally managed to catch one it was after seven. Al had said the Passover Seder would start at six-thirty.

Twenty years ago, when I first came to this island of modern high-rises and skyscrapers, I was amazed to discover that what I considered only mildly entertaining stories in the Bible many people regarded as the basis for the performance of all sorts of tribal rites. Maybe it was I who was strange, but I could not get over how various groups, consisting of so-called sophisticated people, could celebrate three-thousand-year-old fairy tales of uncertain veracity so literally. There were similar practices in my country, but they were all far removed from me. I could not have cared less about them. I never had to relate to any of them at all. But when I heard my relatives here were involved in such observances and rituals, I was shocked. What kind of old-fashioned family had I married into? In Japan I hated that sort of thing and had managed to steer clear of it. And now, ironically, in America I was stuck with it.

Before leaving the apartment, when Al informed us that the Seder would last about four hours, Jon and I had just looked at each other in astonishment. And I had sympathized with Jon by shrugging helplessly. Well, it was already after seven, which meant, at the rate the traffic was crawling, we might not get there for another half hour. Still it would be a long evening. I gazed at the snow, still ceaselessly falling outside the taxi window.

Al looked at me and then at Jon. "The Seder's already long begun, which means we're not going to have to sit for any four hours," he said. Jon and I knew Al felt guilty and was trying to assuage us. We both turned away in silence.

Cars passed our taxi, spewing up crushed snow and ice at us in noisy splashes; snowflakes swirled frenetically before our headlights, as if trying to free themselves from the entanglements of the rays. Then, beyond the snow ahead loomed a steep perpendicular cliff of sturdy buildings, shoulder to shoulder, facing the river. Across the rippling lace curtain of a window high above the street, I saw a human shadow move behind a lamp like a figure in a magic lantern show. There was no color anywhere, just a white curtain of snow and the dull light of a window showing through it.

We got off the elevator on the 29th floor, turned right, and walked over a beige sisal carpet until we came to 29D. At the door we could hear the muffled sounds of choral singing. Al pushed the white round button to the right of the door and the singing stopped. Then we heard the clash of metals as the chain locking the door from the inside was released. The door opened, revealing a slim, handsome woman in her mid-fifties. She wore a black dress and had chestnut-colored hair, cut short around her ears; her complexion was a healthy one, and her full cheeks blended in harmoniously with her other facial features. Al hugged her for a long time and kissed her on the cheek before introducing Jon and me. She was, as I had assumed, Ellen, our hostess.

We walked through the foyer, past a corridor, into the living room. Behind the living room was a dining room that opened off another corridor. Some dozen people were seated there around a long table over which hung a large crystal chandelier. The fragrances of the various perfumes the women were wearing, the smoke of the burning candles, the cooking scents of thyme and bay leaves, overwhelmed me. I suddenly lost my capacity to think. I did not even know in what language to think. It was as if I found myself in a room from which all oxygen had fled.

Whenever I have to go to some new place I have never been to before and have to meet people I have never seen before, I immediately feel that I must surround myself with a fence of double or triple strength. I become like a cat whose fur immediately stands erect, like a hen whose feathers ruffle, because these new people frighten and intimidate me. Who are they exactly, and what are their personalities? All my antennae have to gather information quickly and transmit it to the deepest cells of my brain. I can not rely on verbal input. I have to function as unconsciously as a sweat gland on the skin. Some hidden component of my brain must emerge and take full charge. I became this way after coming to America. I could not rely on language any longer so I had to depend upon this new resource. It was like the self-protective instinct of animals. And in twenty years this part of my brain—or sixth sense, call it what you will—has developed to an extraordinary degree of sensitivity. Even after I began to understand English the fact that there was Ken, who could never talk any language at all, served to sharpen that sense even more.

As soon as the three of us entered the living room, the people sitting around the dining-room table stood, and some of them came out to the living room to greet us, their movement causing the many burning candles to flare. Ellen had taken my overcoat, and I watched as she carried it to a room at the end of the corridor. I did not know these people who were gathering about us, but I shrank back as if I were a hen or a kitten being stared at by leopards licking their lips. I was the only one there who was not a Jew. I was the only one there who was of a small and different race. Jon might have been feeling much the same way, too. But at least he was half Jewish and half Caucasian, making him only half as different as I was.

My hand reached to my neck above the simple brown woolen dress I was wearing, and I realized I had no necklace. The women standing about me were all wearing diamonds and pearls. Perhaps for me to come to such an important festival without an ornament of any sort was impolite. Living with Ken I could never dress nicely in the normal sense. If I wore a necklace, for example, he would reach up and pull it down, scattering it everywhere. When we were going out there was always something to do involving him until the very moment we left the house. I scarcely had the time to even change into a good dress. I became accustomed to that way of living, forgetting about the daily lives of normal people. Jon suffered because of this, too. There was no room in my schedule to instruct him in the proper social graces.

Ellen was busily introducing us to her husband and to her brother and his wife when lo and behold, Sylvia appeared, walking as if on a balance beam, apart from everyone else. In a black dress that looked like a quilted kimono she reminded me of the engravings of the oxen on the walls of the Altamira Caves. Head down, she moved her eyes from left to right until she was directly facing Al. "Hello, Albie, how are you, dear?" she said in a deep low voice and kissed him on the mouth.

I felt the pores of my skin stiffening. But with all the strength I could muster I mangaged to say, "Hello, Sylvia."

She pretended not to hear me. Since Sylvia is not only fat but tall my eyes were at the level of her massive breasts. Unable to establish eye contact, I felt both ridiculous and helpless. This was

38

not the first time I had been ignored by Sylvia, but it still left me confused.

At that moment a small old man with a rosy complexion, in a gray pinstripe worsted suit and a black polka-dotted vermillion necktie, was squeezing his way past Sylvia. The yarmulke covering the top of his head could not hide the fact that he was bald—just like Al. And the craggy outline of his face, the sharp Pinnochio nose, the square jaw that jutted out, was the same as the faces of both Al and his cousin Ben, the pop singer, whom I knew. So this had to be the eighty-three-year-old Uncle Irving, the younger brother of both Al's dead mother and Ben's dead father. He seemed to be enjoying a healthy old age, his blue eyes sparkling with a gentle luster as he opened his arms wide to draw Al, who was ten inches taller than him, into them. He hugged Al, and Al hugged him back, the two men standing there in each other's arms silently until their eyes moistened and they pulled back and studied each other.

Most of us in the room held our breath, as if watching a scene in a theatrical performance. And when Uncle Irving finally spoke it was indeed like a great actor delivering the first line of a famous speech. "Welcome. Welcome, Al," he said in a beautifully modulated soft voice. "How many years is it since we have seen each other? Since before you married?"

"It's twenty years, Uncle Irving," Al said. "I'm really glad to see you." Now tears fell from his eyes, Uncle Irving's too, and they embraced again.

"I think often of your mother," said Uncle Irving, raising his pink face. "But ever since I heard you would be coming this evening, I kept remembering her only as a young schoolgirl. And I dreamed about her all last night."

Al turned to me and Jon, who were lost behind the people beside him. "Uncle Irving, this is my wife, Michi." He pushed me forward with his right hand. "And this," he nodded with his face toward Jon, "is our fourteen-year-old son, Jon."

I was nervous. All these people were watching us, and I would have to talk in front of them. "I have heard about you often from Al," I managed to say. "I am glad we finally can meet." My voice sounded strange to me, unfamiliar, as if it had wandered off on some abnormal tangential pitch. I wondered whether Uncle Irving would be able to understand my Japanese-accented English. Or, to be more precise, my Osaka-accented English. His ears certainly were not used to it. A person his age, I was sure, rarely encountered any Japanese of any kind at all.

Jon followed my cue with an unnaturally stiff face. "I'm glad to meet you," he said and extended his hand to Uncle Irving.

"Welcome. Welcome. It's really nice to see you both. It makes me very happy." He was facing us, still shaking Jon's hand. Then, beaming with joy, his blue eyes still moist, he leaned over and kissed me on the cheek. My heart overflowed with warm emotion. I had come there that evening expecting to find in each of Al's relatives another Sylvia. Instead, I was relieved. Uncle Irving, and those gathered about him, certainly did not seem to have

40

Sylvia's insensitivities. I felt the webs of the network of protective antennae so tightly spun around me loosening.

In the dining room on the long table, which was covered with a cloth of linen lace, three green bottles of Manischewitz wine stood equidistant from each other. But also on the table were a pitcher and basin of white porcelain, which seemed completely out of place, because each setting consisted of Gorham silverware, Dalton chinaware ringed in a light-blue and gold floral pattern and an imposing wine goblet of Waterford crystal. I noticed the rims of the wine glasses were tinged with red, which meant they had already begun drinking.

There were three empty chairs next to Sylvia, and we were led to them. At the head of the table sat our host, Ellen's husband, Heshie, with a white pillow behind his back and a black yarmulke on his head. Ellen brought Al and Jon yarmulkes. Al put his yarmulke on matter of factly, an automatic habit out of his past. But the very perfunctory nature of the gesture distanced him kilometers from me; immediately I felt the alienation of an outsider again. Nor did Jon's hesitation when he was handed his yarmulke escape me. I did not care whether he wore the yarmulke or not. But as the yarmulke still dangled in his right hand, Jon stared at both Al and me with hatred in his eyes. When we lived in New York I would often see pictures of Mayor Lindsay or Governor Rockefeller, in the newspapers or on the TV news shows, wearing yarmulkes as they attended the funeral services of prominent Jews. Jon did not know about

41

these practices, and it never had occurred to me to explain them to him. Besides, I simply never imagined yarmulkes were worn in ordinary homes. No wonder the kid was upset. I did not feel so calm myself. Meanwhile, across the table, Ellen's daughter, a sweet-faced fifteen-year-old girl, and Ellen's twenty-year-old son, a pale-complected but bright-looking student, were observing Jon closely. He could not fling the yarmulke to the floor without an incident. Finally, as if he were chewing on sour poison, he dropped the yarmulke onto his head.

I quickly glanced over the table again. Was this not the same ritual of celebration that DaVinci painted in "The Last Supper"? Was that not a Passover Seder, too, with Jesus sitting at the head of the table? At that time did not Jesus also celebrate the festivals of Judaism?

Diagonally across from me sat Ellen's brother and his wife, both of whom were very fat. Beside Heshie was Uncle Irving, and next to him sat an elegant lady with wavy silver hair, who wore a pink evening dress. In the brief introductions I could not figure out exactly who she was. But Uncle Irving's wife had died long ago, and Al had said something about Uncle Irving having a girl friend. And I now assumed that was her.

Al had told us that we need do nothing but eat and drink but as soon as Jon and I settled back in our seats two small cardboard-covered booklets were passed to us. The booklets opened from the right like Japanese books and had Hebrew running down the right-hand side of each page and English on the left. I felt the same annoying rush of blood flooding my brain as I used to feel at exam time when I saw I could not answer every question on the test paper. In addition, I realized I had not brought my new reading glasses with me, which upset me even more; I cannot even read a menu without them. Anyway, I did not want to waste time on this sort of thing. There were mountains of books I really wanted to read but had been unable to get to all the time Ken was at home. I saw no value in reading ancient tales involving the ancestors of someone else's tribe. Even worse, the reading of these stories would be in the service of religion, and I hated and detested all religion.

"Well, where were we?" asked Heshie. He had black-rimmed glasses and a warm, open face. Sitting straight up in his chair, he picked up a booklet from the table before him. His booklet, like mine, was called *The Passover Haggadah*. Thumbing through it until he found the place he was looking for, he began to read and sing at the same time in a loud reverberating voice. Suddenly it was as if I was listening to Gregorian chanting. I was so startled, I simply stared at Heshie's face dumbfounded, awed by the thought that if you were the head of a Jewish family you might have to have such a voice. When I was a schoolgirl in Japan I always had a difficult time with the music test because the test always involved singing. Would I be called upon to sing here tonight, too? With my voice?

Sylvia, sitting next to Jon, was constantly leaning over him, showing him where the place was in Hebrew. I had already given up trying to figure out where on earth Heshie was reading in any language. Soon my thoughts turned to Ken. I had called the group residence in the morning and asked how he was doing. "Don't worry," I was told. "There are no problems." But Ken can never talk or understand the talk of other people. I too could not speak the words before me or understand the words that were being spoken and sung. None of it had meaning for me. And another surge of blood rushed to my head as I realized Ken was always in this state. When I first came to America I had that abject feeling all the time. Then, gradually, as I began to understand more and more English, it decreased in intensity. Still, I recalled how difficult the week before we put Ken in the residence had been. It was as if, even though Ken could not talk or really understand language, he was fully aware of what was going to happen to him, because of our behavior, our very way of talking.

"Dai dai ennu. Dai dai ennu . . ."

Everyone was singing this song together. The chorus, which my *Haggadah* translated as "It would have been sufficient," had a sound full of vigor and joy. It reminded me of an Israeli folk dance, but one with Russian and German influences rather than Middle Eastern ones. The migrations of these people were echoed in their music. Uncle Irving's voice resonated deeply. He had a lovely voice, lively and energetic, and did not sound at all like an eighty-three-year-old man.

When I first met Al he would sing verse after verse of a song he said was from Gershwin's *Porgy and Bess*. I knew the beat was different from that of European music, and it was different from the American music I was familiar with. I imagined it was a kind of American music I had never heard before. What impressed me most was that Al could remember so many lyrics. Then after we were married Al would often sing something in Hebrew and say, "This is a Chanukah song," or "This is a song sung at Passover." But they would both sound exactly the same to me as the Gershwin song. And I thought: What a strong impression Jewish music makes. Even though Gershwin was supposed to have been greatly influenced by jazz, his music actually seemed much more like the Passover song sung by Al. But the Passover songs I was now hearing at the Seder could not compare to those sung by Al. These were gay and lively and had melodic variations. Al had sung every song off-key in his version of some universal dirgelike tune. Listening to Uncle Irving's singing I understood why there could be musicians among Al's cousins.

The only other person singing out of tune, besides Al, was Sylvia. The black dress she had pushed her globs of flesh and rode halfway up her back as she sat hunched over the table. No matter where she was, Sylvia always seemed set apart from people, misplaced and uneasy. But tonight she was obviously making an effort to smile, instead of frowning as she usually did. I had not seen Sylvia for four years. Since that time, when she visited us in Los Angeles, she had had a hysterectomy and an operation for the removal of some polyps from her intestines, and had suffered a mild heart attack from which she was still recovering. Because of the heart attack, the doctors told her not to overeat and to cut down on her drinking. She insisted that she had not suffered from a *real* heart attack but rather a reaction to some medication she took for asthma. She could still eat anything she wanted without worrying, she told me over the phone, even fatty foods. That explained why her body was more bloated, her cheeks more puffed up, and her skin had an even oilier cast than ever before.

When I first met Sylvia, shortly after I came to America, I was not only shocked, I was disgusted. Out of all the people in this vast country, why did I have to end up with a grotesque sister-in-law of such Amazon proportions? Why her? And with that face! She wore so much makeup around her huge eyes and on her greasy nose that she resembled Oiwa, the disfigured ghost famous in Japanese legend. In addition, she had all the insensitivities of the West and was as fixed and rigid as the stone walls of old New York buildings. I did not know that she represented but the tip of the iceberg of Western ugliness. I only knew that I was upset, that I wanted to be out of her sight and for her to be out of my sight immediately. Why I did not depart, just vanish and disappear then and there, I would later never quite understand. Unless I was so deeply in love with the man sitting next to me... ? Still, should not the strangeness that exuded from Sylvia have hinted of the possibility of a Ken? And if I had simply run away and fled, Ken would never have been born.

"*Rabon Gamliel hoyaw omer. Kol shehlo omar shihlosha divorim . . .*" Heshie read in Hebrew. Al

46

leaned over and pointed out the place to me. But I was busy looking at the opposite page, hurriedly reading the English meaning of the Hebrew. For over three thousand years the ancestors of these people have been looking for freedom. Freedom! Freedom! Liberation! Right on! For me too! I had come to America looking for freedom. My Pharaoh was the conformity of Japanese society, its utter conventionalism, its complete male chauvinism. I came to America fully expecting to find the freedom to paint.

A month ago, just before we placed Ken in the group residence, I tried to wash his hands in the narrow children's bathroom. He grabbed my hair in his large hands and began to pull it. I was afraid that he would actually pull my scalp off. I wondered if prisoners received this kind of treatment. As he pulled my hair with all his might, with hands that covered half my head, I leaned forward toward his chest, placing the top of my head at the level of his chin. Suddenly, he sank his teeth into my scalp. Fortunately, I have a full head of thick hair, and he could not break my skin. But still I could barely breathe as I wiggled about in extreme pain, imploring with a weak voice, "Let me go, Ken. Please let me go." I did not have the strength to pull him off me. And if I had such strength, I still would have wound up losing a great deal of hair. What was going on within his brain, anyway? I wondered. Whenever he had a fit like this, his eyes turned upward, he clenched his teeth, and he stiffened completely. Did he think someone or something awful was attacking him?

He did not always pull my hair straight up; some-times he pulled it an angle and twisted it. Then the pain doubled and my twisted neck would go into spasm. Breathing would become difficult, and I would fear a blood vessel in my brain was about to burst. If he managed to pull out all the hair in his hands would I be left with a bald spot? I was frightened at the prospect but still I would try to loosen his grip without betraying my panic. Until finally, after a long struggle that left me gasping for my breath and my arms completely bloodied and scratched by his fingernails, I would be freed. But under my sleeves there were always scars; they would not fade away so easily.

Last month when I was freed, I was dizzy to the point of almost fainting. But I was also lucky. This was after a urination. A few weeks previously, when Ken had a stomach flu, he became much more frenzied. He had smeared his excrement all over the toilet bowl and onto his underwear. And even with his limited capacity for judgement, he knew he had done something he should not have done, and he felt terrible because of it. So when I came to clean him, he pinched me and then grabbed my hair, which I had just washed that morning, his hands still covered with feces.

If I were a little bigger physically I do not think I would ever have become so worn out. But I had to do everything by myself, shopping, running the house, handling Jon's school problems, in addition to taking care of Ken. I might even have managed to endure everything physically if Ken did not resist so much, draining my nervous system completely. Taking care of a wild boy the size of Ken was usually a man's job anyway. But after Al came down with his heart problem he could no longer do it. We tried employing various helpers and aides, but none of them lasted very long. It was up to me alone to take care of Ken, to thread my way through his rampages, and I became even more run down.

Many people thought I was a fool to keep Ken at home. But there was no place that would take him, until we found the current group residence that accepted him. But who knew how long they would keep him. This vacation could be all we ever would get. This could be it, because at any time they could say "Come and get him," that they could no longer handle him.

The more difficult the child like Ken, the less likely it is for a private institution to accept him in the first place. It means they might have to hire extra help or better-trained personnel to handle him, and they are never sure they can afford that. Particularly when the state government is in the process of changing from a Democratic to a Republican Administration, because that almost always means a cut in the budget for aid to the handicapped and the disabled. So there always would be the prospect of Ken's having to return to our house. I might have found physical liberation for a month, but I knew I would never enjoy emotional liberation as long as Ken lived. No wonder the back of my neck was always stiff.

Just as society as a whole always likes to pretend that children like Ken simply do not exist, so too has Sylvia pretended. Since Jon was born, fourteen years ago, I constantly have had to work like a slave. But not once, not one single time, did she ever offer to watch the kids. Not even one cold winter when we were snowed in in a New York suburb and all four of us came down with the flu did she offer to help. "Oh?" she later said, with matter-of-fact indifference. "You all had the flu? I did not know that." She knew it all right. What did she think we had told her on the phone when she called. And even though she always bought expensive gifts for theoretically normal Jon, in an attempt to bribe him, she never brought Ken a single thing. Not once. She just ignored his existence along with mine. Society and Sylvia ignored Ken and me, and I often thought we both would be better off in hell.

So after finally getting a vacation after all these years, as I say, I was brought to this Seder. And now I had to look at Sylvia, sitting there like a pachyderm, who given her recent medical history could very well become an additional burden for me to bear, another perpetual patient I would end up having to take care of. And, as the Hebrew ceremonial chanting and reading droned on, I suddenly found myself talking to her, addressing her in my mind, in the peculiar Osaka dialect of my native language that comes most naturally to me:

Do you remember when Al and I were first married and lived across the East River in Brooklyn Heights, where there were so many pretty brownstone houses and green tree-lined streets, facing a view of the Wall Street skyline? Our apartment was on the corner of Pierrepont and Henry streets, was it not? And since we did not have enough money to go on a honeymoon, we intended to spend our first night of marriage there. The A & S department store promised us our bed would be delivered by then. We waited all day and finally gave up and had to sleep on the floor in a sleeping bag. Al was delighted by the idea. "Just like a Hemingway novel," he said. And the next morning, after he went shopping for breakfast food in the supermarket, because we could not trust my command of English, the telephone rang.

"Hello, Michiya," a very cheerful voice said in a heavy accent. "How are you?"

I wondered who on earth was Michiya. I was about to hang up the receiver saying, "Wrong number." Only I did not know how to say "wrong number" in English. So no matter who the phone call was supposed to be for, I answered, "Fine." But as I was breathing out the word, some electrical circuit clicked in my brain: *Michiya was the Russian way of saying Michi.* And I realized that my new mother-in-law was the caller.

By that time it was easy for me to say the word "fine." I used that word often. Whenever I met American people, no matter what question I was asked, I would usually answer with that word: "fine." But once I had used my "fine" up, I knew I would have a problem in this conversation.

"What's new?" The next question dropped on me like a stone. Her "new" had a heavy sound, and I heard it as "nu." I could barely decipher it. I looked up at the ceiling, the receiver at my ear, and thought, What can her question mean? "What" is "what." "New" is "new." But "What is new?" What is the meaning? And then, after a long time pondering, *ah!* the meaning "Is something new?" came into my head. So I answered in one word, "Nothing." And I expected she would say goodbye and I would be relieved.

But she came back with, "Where is Albie?" This question I could understand immediately. She always called Al "Albie," referring to her thirty-two-year old son with an affectionate diminutive, as if he were still a child.

I took about a minute to compose an English sentence. "He went supermarket," I said.

"Please tell him to call me when he comes back," she said and hung up. I was breathless even from having to hold such a short conversation. I realized for the first time how much more difficult it is to understand a foreign language over the telephone than talking face-to-face.

Ten minutes later the telephone rang again. I thought I should not answer it. But it kept ringing. So stupid, honest me picked up the phone. Timidly.

"Hello, Mich." A gloomy voice spoke with a sigh full of hate. I cannot explain exactly why, but all of a sudden the receiver felt like one of those rocks we use when making pickles in Japan. "Hi, this is Sylvia," continued this detached masculine voice that sounded as if sputum were still lodged in its throat. In a foreign language the hardest words to catch are names. But yours, Sylvia, I could tell by the tone of your voice. You were calling from your office. You were supposed to be a top-notch editor

52

in a big publishing house, and I thought you would devote yourself to your job and forget about your family. But I was wrong.

"What's new?" you asked me in your clipped New York accent. I was disheartened, because both mother and daughter asked me the exact same question.

But since I had practiced this sentence just ten minutes before, I could answer very quickly this time, "Nothing new." At the same time I knew what to expect next.

"Where is Al?" the question came.

And I was prepared to quickly answer it. "Al went supermarket," I said for the second time that morning.

"Oh, you let him go to the supermarket? When do you think he'll have time to work then?" I heard sounds to that effect, but I could not understand your English completely. Anyway, I thought to myself, Who cares? It was none of your business. But you began to talk continuously, and soon I was at my wit's end trying to follow you. I heard the word "depressed" many times, and I could not understand the meaning of how you were using it. Were you talking of an economic depression? Or something to do with a fall? Maybe you had fallen into the dirt somewhere with your big, clumsy body? But New York City was mostly concrete, and it was difficult to fall into that. Could you have fallen into a sewer and now were telephoning me about it? Or into the dirt of Washington Square Park, which was near your apartment? My brain was like a computer calculating all the wrong answers. But I was in a state of great confusion, and if you cannot understand a foreign language you imagine all sorts of strange things. I did not have the vaguest notion of the diction or jargon you were using. So I kept thinking very hard about that word *depressed*, which you were using over and over again, and about that flat tone in your voice, and suddenly I linked them together: I was living in New York; New York is a big city, and big cities do not have much sunshine. And you were trying to tell me, a foreigner, a stranger in this country and this city, that you were melancholy. I was going to become melancholy or "depressed" myself if I kept listening to you. That could do me in. What on earth did you expect of me? I was a newcomer; I was not a psychiatrist. And as you rambled on I became increasingly frustrated, because I could not say these things to you in English.

When Al came home from the supermarket I told him what little I could understand of our conversation. He said he thought you tended to overuse the word *depressed* to describe yourself because you thought that made it seem as if you were intelligent. And then he got on the phone to you for over an hour. I was amazed. And then in the evening you called for another hour. I was even more amazed . . . the very person who scolded me for taking Al away from his work by allowing him to go shopping. Hypocrite!

This went on every day. My mother-in-law called me once in the morning from her brother's office, where she worked—"What's new?"—without fail. And you called twice a day. What could be new, what could be different for a newlywed couple without children? I could not tell you that we made love last night, could I? But in the bottom of your hearts is that not what both of you knew every morning?

Indeed, I could not understand, at the time, how Americans think and how I was expected to behave and what the proper etiquette was for dealing with a telephone's insistent ringing. I became a telephone phobic. It was just too much trouble having to deal with the calls from my two in-laws in English. Especially since they wasted my time in purposeless conversations. So I decided to put the telephone in the bedroom chest.

I picked Al's drawer. Whenever he left the house I wrapped the telephone in layer after layer of his underwear and undershirts so as to muffle the telephone's *jin jin* ring. If I could not hear it I could not know who was calling, so how could I feel guilty about not answering it?

One day shortly after Al had returned home and removed the phone from the chest it began to ring almost immediately. The caller, of course, was you. "Is Michi out a lot these days?" you asked him.

"No," Al answered with utter but stupid honesty. "She is at home, but she does not want to be bothered, so she puts the phone in the bottom of the drawer." After that, things were really a mess. An ordinary, normal person would have said, "Oh? If she thinks that way she simply should have said so, and I would not call so often—" But you are no ordinary, normal person. You had no idea how much you were disturbing me. Nor did you want to hear about it. "Michi does not love me! Michi does not want to talk to me!" I could hear you screaming to Al over the telephone.

I certainly did not want to talk to you. I could not speak English that well. I did not enjoy staring at the telephone thinking I must make some sound and becoming disgusted at my inability to do so. You could not understand that kind of sick feeling. I wished I could really tell you very clearly in no uncertain terms that I did not like depressed, self-centered people.

From that time on, you implanted an idea in my mother-in-law's head. She was a slow thinker who could easily be a blind follower. If she had had a sounder mind and more faith in her own judgements, she and I would have remained good friends until her death. And not only did you subvert me with my mother-in-law, but also with the people here. With Ellen, for example, I am sure. I could tell when I walked in here this evening that these people were seeing the image of me you had given to them twenty years ago.

Indeed, as I looked across the table at Al's cousins, they still seemed to be regarding me suspiciously, giving me visual third degrees. Why did my husband and sister-in-law have to do this to me? My credo is that of an atheist; the rejoicing of their people was not a cause for my rejoicing. I stared vacantly at the small plates on the engraved silver tray at the head of the table. They contained horseradish and onions, boiled eggs, sprigs of parsley, diced apples and nuts, and the leg bone of a lamb. When the ancestors of the people seated at this table were slaves in Egypt building pyramids, my ancestors were gorging themselves on small mountains of shellfish in Japan. The ancestors of these people were not only enjoined from eating shellfish but also pork. And the chicken and beef and lamb they ate had to be killed in a special ritualistic way, involving special prayers and blessings, so as to be *kosher*. But half of these people, especially those of my generation, nowadays ate anything, whether it was kosher or not. Since there was no true depth to their beliefs, why did they bother to attend this ceremony? But because they all gathered together, I had to suffer. I did not believe in any God; I could eat anything. I certainly did not belong at any religious ceremony. If only my husband could have acted logically and consistently. He considered himself a rationalist. But somewhere in his brain the roots of the nerves were twisted. That was the problem. He wanted to be modern and traditional at the same time. Greedy sentimentalist!

I recalled the trip Al and I took to Egypt in 1962. Ever since I had learned Western history, my greatest dream was to see the Sphinx and the Pyramids. One reason was because pictures of them were on the very first page of my history book. Another reason was that after the Pyramids and the Sphinx we were inundated with so many other Western names that I could never remember any of them.

On the visa applications we picked up at the Egyptian consulate there was a column in which

to list religion. Al and I, of course, were both athe-
ists. But if a country expected everyone to have a
religion, we could well imagine how such a country could be expected to treat people who had no
religion at all. In addition, at this time, shortly
after the Six Days War, a person going to or coming from Israel would not even be admitted into
Egypt. There was no reason for Al to write down
"Judaism" as his religion in that column. Not only
because he did not believe in the religion but also
because it would only create a great problem. So
how to fill out that form? What to put down? We
decided to put down that Al was a Buddhist. What
did they know about Buddhism? But suppose for
some reason Al was asked for proof of his Buddhism? I asked my Christian mother to secure some
statement concerning my Jewish husband's Buddhist convictions from the priest who always visited our house. She did, sending it on to me in care
of American Express, Paris, so Al could have it in
his back pocket by the time we set foot in Egypt.

I remember how hot that desert was in winter,
glittering white sand contrasting beautifully against
the rich blue sky. The Pyramids, drawn in simple,
sharp classic lines, were the very same color as the
desert sand. We ran into a large stone room to
escape the wasps swarming at the entrance in the
strong desert sun. It was the tomb of someone who
obviously had held an important position in ancient
Egypt. We came to a dark corridor where chiseled
on the stone wall slabs, each about the width
of a *tatami*, were engravings of plants, animals,
utensils, and people, who were depicted going about
their daily lives. The members of our tour group,

some of them sighing audibly, gazed with deep admiration at the finely wrought lines. Al may have been resenting the fact that these very tombs could have been the result of the forced labor of his ancestors. A darkly colored, thin Malaysian, in his forties, carrying a black brief case, who had previously introduced himself as a Socialist councilman from Kuala Lampur, asked behind Al's back in the darkness, "Who built this Pyramid?" Al, staring at the engraved rock wall before him, answered without even turning around, "Slaves, of course."

"Slaves?" The councilman screamed as if he had just been stung by one of the wasps swarming about the entrance, and there was terror in his black eyes as they iced over. "I did not come to see things built by slaves! I am a Socialist!" he shouted. "Why on earth are you showing me things built by slaves? Didn't I tell you I wanted to see schools, hospitals, orphanages?" And he lashed into our tour guide as if he had just been asked to view the head of Medusa.

Al tried to calm him down. "You must have taken the wrong tour bus," he said. But the councilman just shook his head and began to wrestle with the guide, insisting angrily that the rest of the tour consist exclusively of schools, hospitals, and orphanages. Al stepped between the two and pulled them apart. Back on the bus, Al quietly pointed out to the councilman that, since the other people on the tour had paid to see the Pyramids and the Sphinx, the tour would have to be completed as advertised.

When the noisy bus arrived at the Sphinx, the rest of us got off to see it, leaving the disconsolate Socialist councilman behind. But we all felt somehow sinful standing before the Sphinx. None of us gazed at it for very long, and we all hurried back onto the bus silently. I remember thinking: *The Pyramids of Egypt and the skyscrapers of New York are both made of stone. Three thousand years stand between them. Were not the people who built the skyscrapers nothing but modern slaves?*

Heshie leaned forward and picked up, from the silver tray, the dish containing the leg bone of the lamb with one hand, while reading from the *Haggadah* he held in the other, his rich voice singing out:

"Pe-sach sheh-ho-yu a-vo-sai-nu o-chlin ba-zi-mahn sheh-base ha-mick-dosh kah-yom. Ahl shoom mah?"

When he finished chanting that paragraph in Hebrew, he read aloud the English translation from the *Haggadah*:

"The Paschal lamb, which our ancestors ate during the existence of the Temple—for what reason was it eaten? Because the Omnipresent, blessed be He, passed over the houses of our ancestors in Egypt, as it is said: 'Ye shall say, it is a sacrifice of the Passover unto the Lord, who passed over the houses of the children of Israel in Egypt, when he smote Egyptians, and spared our houses, and the people bowed themselves and worshipped.'"

Next Ellen's brother picked up the dish with the matzoh on it and read in Hebrew the explanation of its symbolism.

Then when Ellen's son lifted the small dish with

the bitter herbs, the horseradish, and green onion, and read: *"Maw-ror zeh sheh-o-nu o-chlin ahl shoom mah ..."* I could see that everyone was expected to read a paragraph in turn. What would I do when my turn came? There was no way out of it for me. I remembered how, whenever the Buddhist priest who visited our house recited Sanskrit prayers I never understood what he was saying. So how could I be expected to know what was going on now? Al, sitting beside me, following the Hebrew letters, which looked to me like earthworms jumping up and down, pretended not to notice my discomfiture. And if I talked to him, of course, I would be disturbing the ceremony. What I had feared would happen was happening: I was going to become the kind of fool I detest being, the person at the ceremony who does not know the ritual. I began to bear a grudge against my husband, whose mind was now miles away. I stared at him sidelong for a long time, but the indifferent face beneath the yarmulke refused to accept any disturbance, did not show the least hint of concern for the panic Jon and I might have been feeling. I stuck my left hand under the table and pinched him hard on his thigh. He did not move an inch, nor did his face betray a flinch. Instead, Jon, moved his left knee, his right knee, and then his entire body, and, looking down at floor, muttered in a small voice, but with great force, "Shit!" As I had anticipated, he was obviously very upset, too. I regretted that I had agreed to come. Once more I cursed my sentimental husband.

Ruth, Ellen's daughter, was reading the translation from the English side of the *Haggadah* in a high-pitched voice: "We eat bitter herbs because the Egyptians embittered the lives of our ancestors with hard bondage, in mortar and brick, and in all manner of labor in the fields . . ."

Soon Heshie lifted his wine goblet, which had been refilled, and sang out: *"Baw-ruch a-taw a-don-noi elo-hay-nu me-lech haw-o-lawm bo-ray p'ree ha-gaw-fen."* Everyone followed his lead, picking up their own wine glasses and repeating the same words. I did the same, except for the words. I loosened the back of my dress, which had become stuck to the chair, and quickly drank the entire glass of wine. The wine had the sickly sweet taste of Japanese port, but it warmed both my throat and chest.

The white porcelain pitcher of water and the white porcelain basin were slowly passed around the table, starting with Heshie. We all poured water from the pitcher onto our hands as we held them one at a time over the basin. In the *Haggadah*, in English, I read that we were washing our hands before eating dinner. That made sense and was a natural thing to do. But the ritual did not. Perhaps that's why the pitcher and basin still seemed incongruous next to all the fine chinaware and polished silverware set out to celebrate the holiday.

I remembered that when I attended that Seder years ago at Aunt Sarah's home in Brighton Beach I wore a purple angora sweater and tweed skirt and over that, the black wool winter overcoat I had brought with me from Japan. Even though the coat had a silk lining, it must have seemed almost threadbare and shoddy compared with the coats Americans in the East wore during their severe winters. Before going out to Brighton Beach, we stopped at my mother-in-law's apartment to pick her up. No sooner had I entered the apartment than she lifted the bottom of my coat and inspected it, and what I was wearing beneath it, as if I were some five or six-year-old girl. I had been told that Aunt Sarah's husband, Uncle Morris, was a Socialist, so I assumed I need not wear anything showy. And if my mother-in-law was so concerned about how I would dress, then why had she not simply called me beforehand—she certainly knew how to use the telephone—and said, "Dress well tonight."

I was furious with her. Until then, I had thought that sort of nonsense did not exist in America. I felt my future, indeed, looked gloomy. Never had I been so insulted. Not even my own mother had ever stooped to such an action. I never dreamed I would be so demeaned in so modern a land as America. I felt as if the earth had suddenly reversed its course around the sun, revolving thirty times faster than usual in the opposite direction. How dare she treat a woman of thirty with such an utter lack of respect for her individuality and maturity? I was profoundly shocked. It was as if, in Japan, I had been reading all the wrong books. The women of the West were not like Simone de Beauvoir; *The Second Sex* had no relevance. Up until that moment, I think my mother-in-law had carefully kept herself in check by constantly repeating to herself, "I must be very careful in deal-

ing with Michi because I am her mother-in-law."
And by dint of great conscious effort she had been
doing fine; in fact, we had been getting along very
well. And then, as she lifted the bottom of my coat,
our relationship collapsed, crumbling like a bull-
dozed building, tile and stone and wood and plas-
ter everywhere. And the more I think about it,
Sylvia, the more I am convinced that it was your
fault. You were so jealous of the relationship de-
veloping between me and your mother that you
destroyed it by brainwashing her.

Later that evening, at the Seder at Aunt Sarah's
house, I happened to say that the conflicts in the
West between Catholics and Protestants and Jews
all seemed very strange to me, because from the
Asian point of view the Bible was but a single
book and both the Old Testament and the New
Testament were part of it.

Everyone at the table stopped eating. Aunt Sarah,
Uncle Morris, my mother-in-law, and Sylvia just
sat there, their faces twitching, the pupils of their
eyes dilating, as if they had just received electrical
charges from their chairs. I stopped talking, wondering what I could have said that was so terrible,
completely unable to grasp the meaning of their
reactions.

But afterwards, when we returned home to our
apartment in Brooklyn Heights, Al pointed out to
me, "Michi, the Jewish people only believe in the
Old Testament. It is because of their refusal to
accept the New Testament that they have been
persecuted for centuries by Catholics and Protestants. There is no way Jews could ever consider

the New Testament in the same light as the Old Testament." And I realized at once that I did not understand the West when it came to the psychology of the persecuted; in that respect I was still an insular Japanese, insensitive to the rest of the world.

But it was Al who was provincial when it came to the atomic bombing of Hiroshima and Nagasaki. Whenever we discussed the subject he would never accept my judgement that those bombings were war crimes, representing man at his worst. "To kill systematically in a Nazi death camp after routinely inflicting torture after torture," Al argued, "was much more cruel and inhuman an offense than to kill randomly by dropping a single atomic bomb." He made it sound as if the Americans could never have destroyed people as heinously as the Nazis had.

"You have to consider the fact that people killed are people dead," I replied. "No matter how they died, no matter what method was used to kill them, whether they were gassed in a chamber or roasted by radiation in their own homes and died in agony there, the fact of death is the same. They are no longer living. How can you say one way of killing is better or worse than another? People always like to claim that whatever happened to their group was the worst." I had difficulty explaining my position fully because my English was still marred by incidents of childish diction. And when I could not make myself fully understood, I felt completely alienated, forsaken by everybody including my husband—especially my husband. "Which is more of a sin?" I asked him. "To kill six million people or to kill one hundred thirty-five thousand people? Of course, you can always say to kill more people is more of a sin. But then there is no logic and reason in your ethics."

Americans, at that time, simply would not acknowledge in the slightest what a terrible thing their nation had done in dropping the atomic bomb. Most people seemed to think, instead, that the Japanese should thank America for shortening the war by the atomic bombing. Many people who never had known war at all would argue about the war as if it were a sporting event whose score they were still keeping. These people did not know the real pain and hardship and agony of war. Only those people who were there when the atomic bombs fell, only those people who had been in the Nazi death camps, really knew the cruelty and the savagery of war.

It has been twenty years since we had those arguments. Times have changed. Then, there were two Japanese restaurants in all of Manhattan. Now they stand crowded in rows next to each other. One need no longer explain how to use Japanese products; every household is flooded with them. And the anti-nuclear movement has finally achieved international respectability as a pragmatic position. But have we really come any closer in beginning to understand each other's emotions?

Sylvia, too, sings the praises of Japanese products. She likes to tell me how she eats nigiri, tempura, oshitashi. But she still seems unwilling to listen to anything I have to say.

*   *   *

Suddenly the Seder was quiet. Ellen and her daughter rose and went into the kitchen. Dinner would soon be served. I was starting to feel a little tipsy. I had drunk only one glass of wine, but that was on an empty stomach in an overheated apartment. And I was very tired after having walked dozens of blocks during the cold day because of the transit strike. Ordinarily, just one glass of wine, sweet as Japanese port, would not have affected me at all.

But drinking spiced *sake* in Japan on the morning of New Year's Day always made me feel this way, too. My parents would pour less than a glass for me, out of a silver *sake* holder into a small red lacquered *sake* cup, before we formally celebrated by eating *zoni*, rice cake soup. I never liked the formal celebration of New Year's itself. It all seemed so silly to me, having to act like some unthinking puppet in the performance of some assigned role at a traditional ceremony. Days and months inevitably added up to years, which came and went whether you marked their passing ritualistically or not. And who could say exactly on which day any new year began? How stupid people could be!

I had much the same absurd feeling seated at the Seder table. Of course, the dishes and goblets and silverware before me did not have the slightest resemblance to Japanese New Year's paraphernalia. I remembered each individual red-and-black lacquered tray table, bearing a nest of black lacquered boxes in a design of golden plum trees and a red-and-black lacquered bowl for the *zoni*. But even as a small child I resented the unfair, sexist treatment we girls received. Why did my brothers, including those who were younger than me and my sister, get bigger bowls? Why could the men, my brothers and my father, go off to the movies, while we women, my mother and sister and I, had to work so hard, cooking and cleaning for three days running, no matter how exhausted we became. New Year's and how it was celebrated in Japan was no small reason why I came to America by myself. But now, on the table before me, were also arranged the fruits of women's labors. The religion was different, but the same inequities were being practiced in a high-rise apartment in Manhattan.

The gefillte fish appetizer tasted very much like Japanese *tsumire*. Then came chicken matzoh ball soup in the Dalton china bowl. Every tribe has its strange customs and traditions. Before I had a chance to stop him, Al began scooping into his mouth whatever was served. Of course, I could not blame him for being hungry, since it was much later than our usual dinner hour. But his doctor had told him to avoid foods that were high in cholesterol, particularly eggs. And I could tell by its color that the spoonful of matzoh ball he was plopping into his mouth had egg yolk in it. I stared at the remaining portion of the matzoh ball angrily as my heart beat faster, and I kicked Al's heel with my toe. But he went on eating, pretending he had not felt anything. I knew if I so much as uttered one simple sentence, such as, "Do not eat that," his face would redden and he would explode. I did not want that to happen in front of all these people, so I just hunched over further in my

seat, my own appetite gone, and intently observed
Al. After the main course arrived, he wore a frown
between his eyebrows as he held his fork in his
right hand. But he was actually also using the
long, skinny fingers of his left hand. Ken eats in
the same way. Throughout the dinner, Al devoured
whatever was put before him, as if it were truly
his own last supper, taking advantage of the fact
then that he knew I was reluctant to make a scene.
Still, I could not help but shudder as he ate the
skin of the chicken, finally the fat of a piece of
lamb, and a large portion of a cake whose taste
reeked of eggs.

Less than a year before, Al had to go to the
hospital for an angiogram. After he learned the
results, that his right coronary artery was completely blocked, the least little thing was liable to
set off a rage in him. If I cautioned him about the
high cholesterol of a food he wanted to eat, for
example, he screamed, "Shut up! The reason I
have heart disease is because you're always nagging me. Your constant complaining about my eating increases my stress and affects my heart even
more than any food I might eat. If you keep this
up, you are going to kill me!" The purple veins in
his temples throbbed as he shrieked in a dry voice
that strained his throat. His hands would shake,
too, and his eyes glared like a Japanese demon in a
state of fury. Listening to him I feared I was sink-
ing even further into a bottomless pit: Soon I would
have two brain-damaged people on my hands. And
meanwhile, he would be raging on, "I am going to
die soon anyway. So I do not need you giving me

any orders. I am going to go where I want to go, do what I want to do, live as I want to live. I am so angry at you anyway, for being so healthy while I am dying, that I will kill you, too!"

I was so worried about his health. I was doing my best to advise him properly, and he was taking everything the wrong way, just the opposite from what was intended. It was no use trying to take care of him, I decided. I did not want to be killed by this crazy man.

My body felt as if it was being cut in two by a knife when I had to ask Jon to look after Ken while I rushed with Al to the hospital and he was placed in Intensive Care in the Cardiac Unit. But I was really at my wit's end when Al came home from the hospital completely crazed with those unmanageable rages. No longer could I lean on the central pillar of the house. It had rotted away.

Whenever Ken had a temper tantrum, Al became upset. He would even accuse me of causing Ken's temper tantrums. I repeatedly told myself to keep calm, but I was also in a state of exhaustion. All my energy and patience was depleted. I felt so sorry for Jon. I thought of leaving with Jon many times. As it was, life was not worth living. And I was frightened, because I saw no possible way out in the future. I could not depend on Jon; he was too young. Nor was there anybody I could talk to. For the first time in my life I tasted complete loneliness. And nobody could understand my agony —and my anguish—because in front of his friends and outsiders, Al seemed to behave normally.

Yet somehow I found the confidence and resources to go on. I knew I could survive those terrible days. After all, had I not lived through the cruel and savage war, bombings and all?

I turned and looked past Jon at Sylvia, who was stabbing at a slice of lamb on the left-hand side of her plate with her fork. The pinky of her right hand was curled over in the shape of a small mountain, and on her index finger she wore a huge turquoise ring. The slice of meat was thick with fat and gristle. But she did not trim any of it away. Instead, she stopped stabbing at it, snatched it up with the long fingers of her left hand, and shoveled it past her garishly rouged red lips into her large, waiting open mouth. When Ken ate like that there was little I could say or do about it. And now I was helpless too as I sensed the hate I felt for my sister-in-law encompassing my husband. Their gestures were similar; the frowns they wore the same; and the curved lines formed by their shoulders and their backs as they greedily hunched over the table were identical. And, of course, the way they both picked at their food with their fingers. If this was his sister, I found myself thinking, then that was her brother. It was frightening. These people, who could not look after their own health, would call the advice and help of other people "meddling" and "nagging." If they could not follow the regimens prescribed for their illnesses on their own, then why should I have to take care of them? Did they think I could cure their long-abused bodies of their diseases? *Ahorashi!* Utter nonsense. They could do whatever they wanted to do. And if they wanted to be fools, it was not my responsibility.

71

Ra-bo-say n'vaw-raych. Y'hee shaym a-do-noi m'vo-rawch may-a-taw v' ad o-lawm.

The goblets, refilled with red wine, reflected the light of the crystal chandeliers, sparkling above like quartz. I did not have the slightest idea of where they were now reading in the *Haggadah.* But I knew they would eventually get to me, and I tried to keep calm. There were people yet before me. Still, I prayed in my own words, "When my turn comes, just as Jehovah passed over the households of the children of Israel, please let them pass over me here tonight." And since I could not sacrifice a lamb, instead, I spit on my finger and touched my forehead with it, a charm we had used in childhood in an attempt to stop the pins and needles that shot through us when our legs fell asleep.

In the morning, upon awakening, Al used to ask me what color shirt and which pants he should wear. And I never could quite believe that was happening. After all, he was not a kindergarten child. And I would wonder, What's wrong with this man that he asks me such questions? Even though I was a painter, I never wanted to dictate the color or the choice of someone else's clothing. I believed it was very important for an individual to express his own particular taste. In my family in Japan we never asked each other what color clothing we should wear. So I was surprised to discover, in this land that so glorified freedom, somebody who actually asked such questions.

But the first time we had Sylvia over for dinner the puzzle was solved. When I opened the door she did not say "Hello" to me. Without even casting a sidelong glance, she brushed past me, moving in her walking-on-a-balance-beam style into the living room. It was as if she wanted to ignore the fact that I belonged in our apartment at all, let alone as the hostess. Even if a maid had opened the door, in any society it would have been just normal courtesy to greet her with a "Good evening" or a "How are you?"

In the center of the living room, in a green dress that on her looked like a quilted robe, her square jaw protruding, her hands on her hips, her feet planted slightly apart, she reminded me of the Jolly Green Giant in the green peas commercial saying, "Ho-ho-ho." But instead she was saying, "No! No! No!" as she first ordered the sofa to be moved—it belonged nearer the window—and then for Al to change his shirt—the color wasn't for him. She kept insisting until Al finally put on another shirt and we slid the sofa nearer to the window. I soon noticed that whenever Al did try to talk back to her she would scream hysterically. So gradually it became our custom to consult with her, as if we needed permission whenever we wanted to buy something new for our apartment. We became like the slaves who had built the Pyramids in Egypt, and Sylvia was our Pharaoh incarnate.

At that time, I urged Al to choose between me and his sister, because I did not look forward to living the life of a character in a Jean Cocteau or Thomas Mann story. And I now regretted Al's not choosing Sylvia. If he had chosen Sylvia, I need not sit completely bored for four hours. If he had chosen Sylvia, Ken would not have been born.

73

I realized that, deep in his heart, Al never knew what to do about Sylvia. He also never really knew who I was. He must have assumed that because I was Japanese I fit into the usual generalization. I would be subservient to him. I would be obedient to his family. But he was mistaken; generalizations usually are. Any woman who crossed the wide ocean in a small freighter to come to America, no matter what her nationality or race, was an independent woman. And an independent woman could not blindly obey other people forever.

Everyone was lifting their wine glasses and saying something in Hebrew. I grabbed my goblet so quickly I almost spilled the wine, and when they drank theirs, I emptied mine—with gusto. In this ceremony, it seemed to me that you had to drink your wine in one gulp: There was no place in the ritual for just sipping. Since we had come late, this was just our second glass, but for the rest of the people, who had been there from the beginning, it was their third.

"Michi's killing you!"

Didn't you say that to Al? Isn't that exactly what you said, Sylvia? As if you felt that in marrying your brother, who was so important to you, I was denying you of your lover. If Al were married to a white woman, Gentile or Jewish, do you think you would have dared to say such a thing? There would have been an explosive argument, as violent as any tornado. But you took it for granted that I could not argue back with you in English.

What did you mean by "killing you" anyway? That I was actually putting poison in Al's food? Or rather that I was poisoning the further development of his talents, an area you had always assumed was under your jurisdiction and control? Since my English speech was like that of a child, my attempts at it often those of a faltering fool, did you think I was a child and a fool, too? But when one lives in a foreign country and cannot handle the language, one's intuition becomes sharpened to a fine point. One can begin to see all the way through any situation, even to its obverse side. You may have been your high school valedictorian and graduated college summa cum laude, Sylvia, but society does not function along the lines of the chapters in a textbook studiously memorized.

At least Al can thank me for lengthening his life. In the two decades we have lived together, he has eaten far more vegetables and far fewer fatty foods than the average American, because most of my cooking was Japanese. I did not know how to meal-plan the use of such cholesterol-laden Western foods as light cream, heavy cream, whipped cream, sour cream, cream cheese, and creamed cottage cheese.

Oh Sylvia, the hate so long coiled up within, can never untwist!

I leaned toward Al and peered into his *Haggadah*. Then I anxiously turned the pages of mine. Realistically, my having to read in front of all of these people made no sense. But still I had to prepare myself. I tried to figure ahead when my turn would come. Sylvia would read next, and then I would follow. With tired eyes, squinting like a pigeon, I looked over the English two pages ahead.

75

"Oooh-ehen." I heard Sylvia clearing mucus from her throat. Again she made that sound and said, "Why don't you read next, Michi? I don't have a voice right now."

I was concentrating so—studying the section I expected to read, as if it would be some sort of final examination—that I barely caught what Sylvia had said. Only when I heard my name, "Michi," did I lift my head from my *Haggadah* and blink my unfocused eyes into the light, which refracted from the cut glass wine goblets prismatically in every direction.

Al poked me in the arm with his elbow. Blood rushed to my head. "What?" I asked.

"Read," said Al. "You read."

Everyone was watching me intensely. I could feel the heat in their stares, and the blood vessels about my ears were throbbing. I wanted to suggest that we wait for Sylvia to find her voice. Meanwhile, the English letters and the Hebrew characters in the *Haggadah* before me swirled together, forming a single foreign mass—and mess. I wondered what possible religious significance or meaning there could be in my trying to read any of it aloud. "Where?" I asked Al in a small voice.

Al turned the pages of the *Haggadah* from right to left with his index finger and pointed. It was definitely not the section that I had tried to rehearse. Somehow Sylvia always found a way to be mean to me. And the two glasses of wine I had drunk did not make things any easier. My voice quivering, my face flushed, I resigned myself to having to pick at the dancing alphabets. "O eternal God ... " I began to read as I heard Jon mutter, "God!" into the tablecloth. He knew he would have to read after me.

The room became very quiet. I was the object of concentrated curiosity as they all strained to listen to my combination of Japanese-accented English and Anglicized-Hebrew. Even though I have lived in America for twenty years, I still cannot pronounce distinctly the difference between "r" and "l" and "f" and "v." Hearing my own small voice reading sanctimoniously aloud filled me with loathing and self-hate. What were the meanings of the words I was allowing to come out of my mouth? What kind of a hypocrite had I allowed myself to become? At the same time, I was bashful and confused. I suddenly realized I had skipped a line. Should I stop and start over? Or should I just continue?

I decided to wade on: "... Thou freed us when we were slaves in Egypt; thou sustained us with food in time of famine; and in plenty didst thou nourish us. From the sword didst thou deliver us, from pestilence didst thou save us; and from disease and raging sickness didst thou relieve us. Hitherto thy tender mercies have supported us, and thy kindness hath not forsaken us. O eternal God, please forsake us not in the future ..."

In Japan, despite not being a Christian, I was sometimes asked to recite prayers in the Bible class I would attend in order to improve my English. I hated being forced to utter words dealing with beliefs and convictions that were unacceptable to me. Playing the role of the hypocrite has always been intolerable for me. The people at the Seder table were probably wondering why I had not converted to Judaism, like Marilyn Monroe and Elizabeth Taylor. For them, no other religion could have any possible validity. This exclusivity, this clannish conviction that they alone were the sole repositories of the ultimate truth, is something found not only in Judaism but also in Christianity and in Islam, and in the end they often killed each other because of it. In the West, ideologies and theologies traditionally proselytized; unable to leave foreign cultures alone; resulting inevitably in imperialism, evangelism, and even in Nazism.

Sylvia was leaning back in a red velvet wing chair. She had just lighted a fire in the fireplace of the living room of her already overheated apartment. She had on a blue dress of a heavy fabric imprinted with a floral pattern of red roses. In one hand she held a lighted cigarette; with her other hand she rubbed her oil-slick shining black hair. Her knees were set wide apart, and beneath the short hemline of her dress her fat thighs showed all the way up to her crotch. Seated on the sofa in the corner of the room, I was amazed. I had never seen any woman sit so carelessly, not even in the West. I could never imagine any woman sitting that way in Japan.

"We are chosen, Al," Sylvia was saying, exhaling the smoke of her cigarette through her elephant-tusk-like nostrils. "We are the chosen people of Jehovah. That is why we are superior to all other

tribes." Her fat, jowly cheeks trembled, as if she
had become Moses himself, fatigued by the descent from the mountaintop.

There were only three people in the room. The
"we" obviously referred to two of them, Sylvia
and Al. Just as obviously, the "we" did not refer to
the third person, me. I was not "chosen." In other
words, I was "unchosen."

Still newly married, I stared at Sylvia dumbfounded, because it was not the first time I had
heard the term "chosen." American missionaries
visiting Japan frequently used that word, most
particularly Billy Graham. The first time I heard
him say "chosen" I turned to a friend and said
indignantly, "Are we supposed to be so low that
God never chose us? That's ridiculous! What an
arrogant and self-centered notion these people have!
The very idea of calling themselves 'chosen!' 'The
navel boiled the tea,' as we say. How incredible!"
We laughed a great deal over it. But in the West, it
seemed, people actually did consider themselves,
as a matter of course, "chosen." Jews boasted that
they were the "chosen;" Christians boasted that
they were the "chosen." No wonder the "chosen"
were always trying to destroy the other "chosen."

Westerners traditionally assign a superiority to
themselves over others. Whatever they are doing is
always right, so everybody else has to do it, too.
They never seem to have the slightest doubt either. Evidence of such absolute certitude now lay
before my very eyes. Still, I was appalled to hear
this fat slob say she was "chosen." Was she completely insensitive to the discomforting feelings I

might have as a shiksa in the same room? Or did she know exactly what she was doing, fully intending to put me down as much as she could?

Anyway, the great God, Jehovah, was in deep trouble, I decided, if Sylvia was his "chosen."

"U ... hen ... hen ... hen," Sylvia coughed, her napkin to her mouth. "I can read now." Her head nodding, she began to read the Hebrew with the proud elation of the "chosen," the top student in the class, fully prepared to take on the textbook assignment. Her very manner banked the fires of my twenty-year anger, intensifying it to the point where I wondered if I could suppress it any longer.

Next it was Jon's turn, and Sylvia found the page for him, pointing out the place with a long white finger, incongruously slender in comparison with the rest of her body. Jon said, "Oh shit!" under his breath and proceeded to read the English in a dull monotone, his voice as flat and repetitive as a goose's honking, coldly ignoring all possible meaning, variation, and emotion.

Even though I dedicated myself to the care of Ken with all my heart, he could never understand what I was trying to do. He literally bit the hand that fed him. But the bruises inflicted by his pinching, the pain caused by his pulling out my hair, only made my sadness greater than my anger. And no matter how severe the pain I had to endure because of him, the despair of letting him go was even keener. If the small residential facility he was in now did not work out, then he would have to go into one of those snake-pit state hospitals. Or we would have to take him home again. But what could I do with my skinny arms? I was not made of iron or steel.

But Sylvia was sitting there stolidly, as if she were waiting for her turn to be taken care of. In fact, she once told Al that if Ken stayed in residential placement she might visit us and look into the possibility of moving permanently to Los Angeles. Although she never has shown the slightest smidgin of sympathy or feeling of warmth for me, would I be expected to take care of her, just because she was my sister-in-law, in case something happened to her? Because I would not. Never. Not in a thousand years. Not even if she came to me, begging on bended knees. But still, the possibility of having to deal with such an agony awaited me. How could I ever get out of the tunnel if I could not see any light at the end of it?

People are all the same. Utter fatigue undermines the very existence of love. Al blamed me for his illness without considering my feelings at all. So I began to think only of protecting myself. My mind was tired, my body exhausted. What I needed was a long period in which to convalesce. At the moment it seemed impossible to ever regain my lost life. I wanted to sleep ten hours every night, but at my age found myself waking up after less than six hours. Time lost in one's youth is time lost forever. Yet I kept dreaming somehow of having the same kind of life as other people. But the world of a de Beauvoir was as inaccessible to me as the moon a dog at bay might bark at. There was not enough wisdom or guile in all the world to solve my problems.

Unable to bear the anguish of my depressing—
yes, "depressing"—thoughts, I quietly pushed my
chair back from the table as Heshie explained the
song in the *Haggadah* they were about to sing:

"This is a children's folk song. It begins with the
buying of a goat for two *zuzim*, which was very
little money. But listen to the song carefully. It
seems to tell the story of how the goat was devoured by a cat that was bitten by a dog that was
then beaten with a stick and so on and so on. But
actually, in point of fact, it is the story of the long
history of the Jewish people."

I reached down with my right hand and picked
up my black leather handbag from the foot of my
chair and, placing it on my knee, turned my body
to the right. I slid my feet back into my black
pumps and rose, looking downwards. Al lifted his
eyes from his *Haggadah*. "Where are you going?"
he asked.

"Bathroom," I said. And as casually as possible I
slipped away from the table while Heshie was
continuing: "Israel, you see, was first conquered
by Babylonia. But then Babylonia was defeated by
Persia, and Persia was overrun by Macedonia, and
on and on. . . ."

As I put on the bathroom light, a fan immediately
snapped on, too. The wallpaper was of an Indian
antique design, and the mirror had many bulbs on
it, like in an actor's dressing room. After I closed
the door behind me, the fan's noise cut off all outside sounds. I looked at my face in the garish mirror.
It was the face of a forty-nine-year-old middle-
aged woman, flushed with alcohol, further reddened

because of the hot room temperature. No matter how I turned my face about, trying to catch the most favorable light, I was shocked to find that the face not only did not look as young as I wished it to be, but also did not look as young as I had assumed it to be. It was as if the words Sylvia had said to Al twenty years ago, *"Michi is killing you!"* had plunged into my heart with the opposite effect; the person who was being killed was not Al, but me!

I was so frightened by the appearance of my face in the mirror that I wondered whether I was still living or not. I rubbed my right hand over my cheek to make sure. Yes, I was alive. And I had to take good care of the short remnant of the rest of my brief life. I had given twenty years of my life to Al and his family. But that was all. I would not sacrifice the purpose for which I was born. My life was too precious for that. I would get out. I could leave. I could go.

It would be easy. No one need notice. And outside was not the desert or the sea, like in the Bible and the *Haggadah*. There were taxis and planes. In one way or another, I had to get away from this family. Otherwise, my whole life would end up in bondage and servitude. The powerful hands I used to paint with had better things to do than just take care of other people.

I felt my heart beating loudly. Soon my whole body was pulsating nervously, as if it all had become part of one enlarged heart. And I was burning everywhere, on fire down to the soles of my feet.

I turned off the bathroom light and, silently as I
could, walked down the corridor to the bedroom,
where I found my overcoat. I put it under my left
arm, so that when I passed in front of the dining
room, in case I was observed, my body would
shield the bulky coat from view. Then, as noncha-
lantly as possible, I walked briskly down the corridor, looking straight ahead, like a cat who had
found his game and was about to pounce on it.

Heshie's voice, leading the singing, shouted
encouragement:

"Chad gad-yaw, chad gad-yaw
D'za-been a-baw bis-ray su-say
Chad gad-yaw, chad gad-yaw."

"My father bought me a goat for two *zuzim.*"

"Va-a-saw shun-raw, v'awch-law I'gad-yaw
D'za-been a-baw bis-ray su-say
Chad gad-yaw, chad gad-yaw."

"A cat came and ate the goat my father had
bought me for two *zuzim.*"

"Va-a-saw chal-baw v'naw-shach l'shun-raw
d'a wch-law l'gad-yaw
D'za-been a-baw bis-ray su-say
Chad gad-yaw, chad gad-yaw."

"A dog came and bit the cat, which had eaten the
goat my father had bought me for two *zuzim.*"

I put my handbag and coat on the floor and
unchained the door, my shaking hands somehow
making no sound. I turned the knob to the right
quietly and opened the door, as if I were a thief.
Then I picked up my coat and handbag and walked
out quickly, but slowly and carefully closed the
door behind me. In the hallway, on the beige sisal

carpeting, I lay down my handbag and poked my hands through the sleeves of my coat and then picked up my handbag again and walked as fast as I could toward the elevator. The singing, seeping out the door into the hallway, seemed to be celebrating my departure; at the same time, it sounded as if it were running after me, trying to catch me.

When I stepped out of the elevator on the ground floor, I forced myself to smile, as if only in that way could I pass a last remaining barrier. Wearing that frozen smile, I nodded to the doorman and asked him to get me a taxi.

He pushed open the heavy front door of the apartment building, and I followed him out. As I waited on the gray sidewalk, the cold wind blowing in from the East River hit my flushed cheek, and I felt refreshed. My steaming breath gleamed against the dark street. I looked up at the sky and inhaled deeply. The snow had stopped; the clouds had disappeared, and there was a full moon in the cold night sky. The lights of the apartments in the housing complex on Roosevelt Island showed through the dead branches of trees, twinkling like gemstones. Manhattan again seemed to me like the island of hope it was twenty years ago when I first arrived here. Emanating from someplace—I could not tell where—were the fragrances of the American Pharmacy.

I would go to Elaine's apartment in Greenwich Village, I decided. No man lived there; I need not strain my nerves. And tomorrow I would think about my future.

I felt a generation younger as I hurried toward

tt.

Foumiko Kometani

the taxi. The doorman, waiting with his gloved hand on the opened taxi door, smiled and said, "Have a good night, Madam." I gave him a dollar, and the door closed behind me.

A Guest
from Afar

While staring out her kitchen window at the vast Pacific Ocean, at last calm and a deep velvet-blue, Michiko ties the bowstrings of her white cotton apron behind her back. On one side of the L-shaped, white tiled kitchen counter before her squats an electric rice cooker. On the other side of the sink stands a toaster, and beside it on the L leg of the counter, which separates the dining alcove, sits a white telephone. Above the sink are four oak-paneled cabinets, their white ceramic handles staring down at her like two pairs of glaring eyes.

Additional cabinets and rows of drawers line the counter. Across from it, along the opposite wall, is another white tiled counter, four silver-rimmed electric burners embedded in it, flanked on one side by a huge copper-tone refrigerator and on the other by a built-in oven with opaque doors, framed in the same oak paneling as the kitchen cabinets. Overhead, in the center of the ceiling, is a fluorescent lighting fixture encased in a white plastic hood that always reminds Michiko of a Go board upside down.

It is still the middle of the day, but she turns the wall light switch on. Now the entire kitchen takes on a modern luster. More important, she can better see what she is doing. First she looks out the window again, this time at the bougainvillea vines, thorny and red at the tips, coiling around a redwood fence. But there is no sign yet of the buds that any day now will burst forth into flaming vermillion blossoms.

Ken is really very lucky that the rains have stopped, Michiko thinks as she gazes out past the bougainvillea at the ocean, that the three weeks are finally up and he can come home today. Ken is her thirteen-year-old brain-damaged son, who has recently gone to live at BTC, the Behavior Training Center, a special residential training facility for the brain-damaged, whose rules precluded any home visits during his first three weeks of placement. The incessant rains that were lately making Michiko feel mouldy to the very marrow of her bones seem to have ended; for February, the ocean is unbelievably blue, and the sky is high and clear, with only a few white clouds, floating by near the horizon. The promise of afternoon sunshine is in the air. After an eight-month dry spell the rainy season had come late to Southern California this winter, with more rain than usual, as if to make up for its tardy arrival. In nearby Topanaga and Mandeville and Laurel Canyons, wherever the brush fires had raged during the past two years, the almost daily deluges caused home-destroying landslides. And just north of Michiko's house, too, the Pacific Coast Highway was constantly closed because of falling rocks, the traffic re-routed out through the valley and the still-navigable canyons. The problems of the rainy season were all too familiar to Michiko, their catastrophic nature in particular reminding her of Japan. But now, peering out at the limitless expanse of the blue ocean, she can almost physically feel her spirits rising; the very notion that these very same waters wash up against the shores of her native land, so many thousands of miles away, always gives her a reassuring sense of peace and serenity.

Modern American kitchens are not designed for diminutive Japanese women like Michiko. The counter is just too high for her; as she peels potatoes, she has to extend her elbows and stand on her toes and lean up against the cabinet doors on the side in order to balance herself. She goes to the refrigerator and removes the *konnyaku* that comes packaged in a white plastic container filled with water. The only *konnyaku* she can get in Los Angeles has a beige shine and lacks the gray, black-flecked natural texture of the *konnyaku* back home. Michiko unpacks two blocks of the gelatinous *konnyaku*, shakes the water from them, and on the cutting board that slides out from the counter, cuts the *konnyaku* in two and then halves them again into smaller triangles. Next she runs water into three pots—one for the potatoes, one for the *konnyaku*, and one for the broth, or essence—and sets them onto the electric burners. Into the broth she will later add the boiled potatoes and the cooked *konnyaku*. Michiko works swiftly, slicing and chopping the ingredients; she is anxious to have everything cooked and flavored before leaving.

The digital clock on the oven door shows 12:45. Al, Michiko's husband, who is a writer and works in an office nearby, has promised he will be back for lunch by one o'clock so they can leave as early as possible to pick up Ken. Three weeks earlier, when they left the house at three-thirty to drive Ken out to the BTC residential facility in the San Fernando Valley, they found the entrance ramp to the San Diego Freeway at Sunset Boulevard already jammed, the traffic on the freeway below barely moving, and it had taken them well over an hour and a half to get there.

But it had taken them much longer than an hour and a half to reach the decision to place Ken there, months and years in fact. They first discovered the existence of BTC some two years before, while shopping around for a course of action reserved for some vague and distant future. The facility had just opened and everything was fresh and clean and spanking new; in addition, it was located in an ordinary tract house, which gave it an attrac-

92

tive homey quality. But the fact that it was in the Valley, where the summers can become unbearably hot, discouraged Al and Michiko sufficiently to make them start thinking seriously of opening their own "residential school" somewhere along the coast with its more comfortable climate. It was then that Michiko realized that the very same geographical and regional prejudices she experienced growing up in Japan existed in California. Just as people in Kobe and Osaka tended to put down Kyoto-ites as being unpleasant and cheap and miserly because they lived in an area that was so hot in the summer and cold in the winter, Angelinos who resided on the West Side would stigmatize and castigate Valley dwellers in the same way. And, indeed, housing was much more reasonable and affordable in the San Fernando Valley, with its desertlike temperature extremes, than near the ocean. There were even Westsiders who resented the fact that Valley dwellers were bona fide residents of the City of Los Angeles. So when it came time to consider alternate living arrangements for Ken, Al and Michiko were aware that an anti-Valley prejudice had already somehow taken root in the back of their minds.

But during the past summer Ken had grown a great deal, suddenly and unexpectedly shooting up past his mother, his lean body also filling out. Al and Michiko, both of whom were slight in size, had known that such a day would come, but had not looked forward to it. Nor had they anticipated that such a day of reckoning would come so soon. But once Ken started to grow, it was as if nothing could stop him. They had no idea a child could grow over a foot in less than a year. No, that was not quite true. They did have an idea, a very good idea. After all, Ken's fourteen-and-a-half-year-old brother, Jon, had just undergone a similar growth spurt, making him taller than Michiko and nearly as tall as Al. But they just had not wanted to think about Ken in terms of growth. In fact, Michiko realized that if Ken were a normal child she would have viewed his growth spurt as she had viewed Jon's—with joy and pride—a bamboo shoot flourishing in her very own garden. Indeed, if Jon had not grown that dramatically, she might have had cause for concern and worry. But as a mother, she could not help but wish the opposite for the developmentally disabled Ken, because the longer he remained small and babylike, the longer she could continue to care for him at home.

On rare occasions—about once a month—Ken was able to manage a few words of screechy birdlike speech. For example, he might suddenly say, "Iwannaeat," like a one-word song played at the wrong speed on a defective turntable with a worn down needle. Otherwise, the only sounds he would utter in his efforts to communicate were meaningless "eehs" and "oohs" and "ohs," whose constant repetition would grate upon the ears like the keening of some lost animal. And then, as if sensing with an utter frustration that people did not understand what he was feeling or thinking, Ken would proceed to throw a temper tantrum. During such a tantrum, he would pull at Michiko's rapidly graying hair and scratch her face and pinch her wrists. He also kicked the floor, punched holes in the walls, and flipped over tables. That summer Ken had become so big that the diminutive Michiko was simply no longer a match for him, and he knew it.

Ken also frequently suffered from insomnia. During the day, he just did not get the physical exercise necessary to tire the body of a growing boy. And then at night, unable to sleep, he would jump up and down on his bed, shouting and keening into the dawn, keeping the rest of the family wide awake, making Michiko feel each morning as if she had spent the previous night a prisoner in an Occidental torture chamber.

One afternoon toward the end of summer, just as Michiko was reaching for a *daikon* in the produce section of Gelson's Supermarket, the hand of Margaret Davis fell upon her arm. Margaret also had a developmentally disabled son, Casey. Michiko knew she was caught, because once Margaret started to yak it would be a good thirty minutes before she was finished. And Michiko had so much to do before Ken returned home from his special school. The words from an old Japanese children's song, *"Toryanse! Toryanse!"*—let me pass—ran through her head, and Margaret squeezed Michiko's arm even harder, as if she sensed the getaway Michiko was plotting. Margaret was a plump woman in her mid-forties who wore her blond hair pulled back tautly from her round face and rouged her thick lips beyond their natural boundaries. Impervious to her surroundings, she immediately began to issue a progress report on Casey, her

95

large mouth open wide, like a fanatic evangelist preaching the glory of Christ. But at the same time, her beautiful, calm blue eyes shone with a strange sadness, belying the loud and powerful voice, which echoed in Michiko's ears as if a public address system had just been turned on full blast in the produce section. A year ago, Margaret had placed Casey in the BTC facility, where he was receiving an intensive program of behavior modification, Skinnerian techniques applied as if BTC were Walden itself. Michiko patiently pretended to listen, unable to close her ears, with the *daikon* in her right hand, her arm still held hostage. If only Margaret did not have such a loud voice, she thought, she might manage to exude an air of elegance and gentility. But that voice, that crude, vulgar voice was rasping out things Michiko could barely believe. Why did Americans always have to proselytize? They were forever trying to talk you into doing exactly what they had done, to impose their values and belief systems upon you. But after twenty years in America, Michiko was skeptical to the core. Especially when it came to the subject of Special Education and theoretically beneficial programs. She had read enough and heard enough not to believe a single syllable of any syllabus.

As Michiko watched Margaret's broad back finally move away, she placed the *daikon* into her shopping cart and reached up to the greenhouse cucumbers, tightly wrapped in plastic, inspecting them for size and firmness. She thought over Margaret's words and recalled her reputation, in the local school district's Special Education division, as a most picky parent, impossible to please. She was never satisfied with any school or classroom for Casey for very long. He averaged more than one change of school a year, not to mention all the classroom and program changes within the various schools themselves. But just now Margaret had been bursting with nothing but praise for BTC and the way Casey was improving there.

Michiko remembered Casey as being even more severely disabled than Ken. He would lie on the floor, rolling and staring into space like a drunkard passed out on the street. He chewed his food with his mouth wide open, dribbling it down onto his chest. He slurped liquids like a dog lapping its water, making the same sounds, his eyes darting from side to side, never calm and peaceful and at rest. His head was a relief map of lumps and bruises caused by his constant head-banging against walls and floors and furniture; and there were self-inflicted bite marks all over his hands and wrists and elbows. Casey had bitten himself so often that the skin around the bites was flaky and dry, as if a layer of mold had grown over them.

Before leaving the produce section of Gelson's, Michiko decided that it might be time for her and Al to look at BTC again. After all, as she told Al that evening, just as Margaret would give up on every school and every teacher for Casey, each teacher and each school until now had given up on Casey. But evidently that had not happened in the case of BTC. So a few days later they drove out to the Valley to see for themselves the miracles Margaret had been talking about so messianically and fervently.

Michiko could not believe her own eyes; all of her previous doubts and suspicions about BTC were immediately dispelled. Casey, of course, was still unable to speak, but otherwise he seemed to behave very much like a "normal" child. Casey stood tall, his eyes met theirs directly, and he stretched his hand straight out to shake hands with them.

Michiko turned to Al. For once in his life he was speechless. They quickly agreed to place Ken in BTC as soon as possible, in the hope that he might be as successfully transformed as Casey. The staff-to-child ratio at BTC was one-to-one, which seemed to assure Ken's safety; in addition, with a concerned parent—the mother of one of the children in the residential facility—as director, it seemed they would surely be spared the fear of brutal beatings and terrible rapes, which they had so often heard stories about in connection with group residences and institutions. They also very much approved of the facility's policy on the use of drugs: None. No tranquilizers, no sedatives, no psychotropic drugs were ever part of the protocol.

Al and Michiko were also thinking of both their own physical health and the well-being of their marriage: In the end, living with a severely handicapped child could destroy everything. Caring for Ken, day in day out, had already ravaged their lives; they were badly in need of a break—or respite—from Ken. So the changes they saw in Casey were like a beacon of light that seemed to show them the way back from the very edge of despair. They had recently talked of starting a facility of their own. But that would have been, as the Japanese say, like making a rope after finding a burglar in the house. It was simply too late for such a project. But now they could fervently hope that Ken's behavior might improve as miraculously as Casey's had.

Michiko often thought she was part of the problem when it came to taking care of Ken. If only she were a little younger, or stronger, or just bigger, she would blame herself with her Japanese sensibility, she might be able to keep Ken at home for a year or two more. But there was just nothing she could do about the problem once Ken had begun his adolescent growth. While his brother Jon, except for his thick, lacquer-black Japanese hair, looked almost like a Westerner, there was no doubt about Ken's Japanese heritage, facially. But his long-limbed body, with his arms dangling down his sides and long legs, was definitely that of a Westerner. And since Al's father had been over six feet, there was no telling where it would all end, exactly how tall Ken would eventually become. With Al already fifty-two years old and Michiko herself forty-nine, only a miracle would bring forth any growth spurts for either of them. "I have to try everything," Michiko said, to justify the separation to herself. "And if placing Ken in BTC now makes taking care of Ken easier in the long run, then it will be well worth it."

After lunch, Michiko goes to the bedroom, where every available inch of wall space is lined and cluttered with books, to change her clothes. She puts on jeans and an emerald-green sweater. She does not need a coat today; it will not rain, and the sun has broken through the morning fog. She dabs her palms with violet-scented toilet water and rubs her hands onto her face. Her fair skin sets off the emerald-green well. Michiko has an ordinary face. Her only distinctive feature, and she would be hard-pressed to call it "distinctive," is the lazy but graceful arc formed by each of her widely separated eyebrows.

Michiko looks out her bedroom window at the palm fronds swaying beneath the calm cerulean blue sky, and she cannot help but recall that Ken's BTC home is on an asphalt boulevard wide enough to accommodate six lanes of passing Cadillacs. Across the boulevard is a university campus girded by trees not yet sufficiently grown to suggest the woodsy area intended. Michiko, knowing she should not set her expectations too high, still wonders how much Ken has progressed during these past three weeks. As his mother, it is only natural for her to dream that his improvement has been nothing short of miraculous.

She is so anxious to get to see Ken, she cannot keep still. As long as we are going, she tells herself, we might as well leave as soon as possible. She returns to the living room and is annoyed to find Al lying on the living room couch, the morning newspaper spread in front of his face. Americans are so relaxed, she thinks. They take so much time to do anything. As a Japanese, by force of habit she almost automatically does things quickly, efficiently, methodically, getting them over and done with as soon as possible. This is a source of constant conflict with Al. But perhaps it is simply a gender difference. Or is it not so much that she is Japanese but that Al is an American? Yes, she decides, it is Al's Americanness, his lazy laissez-faire Americanness, that is at fault.

"Remember when we brought Ken there? It was an ordinary weekday, not even Friday, but still the freeway was packed, bumper to bumper. Don't you think we better leave soon?" Michiko urges her still reclining husband, both impatience and frustration tinging her Osakan-accented English.

"Yeah, I guess so." Al rises slowly from the couch like a sleeping bird being torn away from his nest. He takes his ocher corduroy hat from the coffee table and jams it over his balding head, then reaches down beneath his hand-knit red sweater into the pockets of his ocher corduroy slacks and comes up with a large pair of sunglasses. He removes his reading glasses and rubs his nose before replacing them with the sunglasses. Then wordlessly, as if wrapped in his own thoughts, he leads Michiko out to the driveway and into their burgundy Honda Accord, where almost immediately the scent of Michiko's violet perfume begins to spread gently throughout the car.

Palm trees line both sides of their concrete-paved street, white in the rays of the midday sun. They drive past Palisades High School, turn onto Sunset Boulevard, and drive through the local business area until they reach a winding stretch of road lined on both sides with tall eucalyptus trees, transplanted from Australia years ago. The trees now flourish as if they were native to the California soil, their scent—like a rich mixture of burnt incense and lavender—drifts along the boulevard, their drooping branches that send out long thin leaves, shiny white in the breeze, shade the road. With their bark peeling off as they hover over the boulevard, the trees remind Michiko of a long line of elderly people.

After the fork where a turnoff leads to Will Rogers Park, Al and Michiko follow the bend of Sunset up the hill to the Riviera, and a bright sky opens up before them. Beneath it are spacious carpets of green lawns, huge gardens containing zinnias, salvia, begonias, bachelors' buttons, roses, camellias, birds-of-paradise—flowers, Michiko could never imagine finding in Japan, let alone on the East Coast of America, during the winter. But these flowers are planted with such precision that they strike Michiko as disturbingly artificial. Indeed, there is not a shred of natural beauty to these gardens. Looming behind them, Michiko sees many large homes of different styles and varying shapes, each with a distinctive characteristic of its own, assembled together as if for some exhibition at a trade fair. Beside a Spanish style home, its patio garden and courtyard girded by a white stucco fence and a cast iron black grille gate, for example, is a white New England style house with French white-framed windows. Next to it lies a sprawling California ranch style home, its roof covered with simple shakes but its huge, deep-red, Asian-looking doors bedecked with so much gold trim that

Michiko half expects the Mikado, or some such potentate, to come flying out of them at any moment. And she cannot help but wonder if the people who live in those homes have any of the every day—let alone the special problems—she and Al have.

Emerging from the Riviera they pass an aircraft-hangar-like building, which is actually Paul Revere, the neighborhood junior high school Jon attended. Then, after a canyon road and after climbing another winding hill, they come into an area studded with apartment buildings. The traffic becomes heavier, and they find themselves not only among passenger cars but big yellow school buses; small dull-colored delivery pickups; motorcycles; a cement truck with a grey and yellow stripe that twirls before them like a top; a maroon van whose sheets of display windowpanes reflect the bright sun; a paint company's truck, loaded high with large cans of paint and stain, and folded canvas sprayed and spattered like the work of Jackson Pollack, red, white, yellow, green, blue—brilliant colors that come shooting into Michiko's eyes while the blare of horns and the piercing sounds of brakes screeching fill her ears. She looks past the mass of vehicles jamming the road at the sidewalks lining either side and once more notes the phenomenon of suburban Los Angeles living: There is not a single solitary soul out walking. Not even a dog.

At the corner, where a tall cylinder-shaped Holiday Inn rises on the left, Sunset Boulevard crosses the San Diego Freeway. San Diego itself lies some two hundred miles to the south along the San

Diego Freeway; Al and Michiko turn north onto the Freeway in order to head out to the San Fernando Valley. The freeway is uncrowded, the traffic flowing smoothly. The road, because of the recent rains, is not bone dry with desert dust seeming to hover over it the way it usually is, but there seem to be more potholes than Michiko remembers.

She cranks her window open an inch, and the sudden burst of incoming air, carrying the sound of squealing tires, displaces the scent of her perfume with the smell of automobile exhaust. Michiko looks out the window at the rising mountains and then turns her thoughts inward. She reviews in her mind the million things she wants to do for Ken when he gets home, starting with simply taking him for a walk along the bluff with Al, Ken trailing behind them and then suddenly prancing ahead of them with a hoop and a holler and then stooping down to pick up a clump of grass to inspect. She turns and studies Al. His hands are pressed down on the wheel, his eyes fixed on the road. Usually, when he is driving, he is a steady stream of chatter, and she becomes nervous as he turns his head to look at her while he talks. But now he is unusually quiet. Is he thinking about all the things he wants to do with Ken, too?

Michiko remembers the day three weeks ago when she and Al brought Ken to the BTC residence. Jon had asked to go along with them, so they had waited for him to return home from school before leaving. Jon, in his first year of high school, was beginning to show a caring and sensitive side of his personality that he had never revealed before. The four of them boarded the same four-door Accord: Al in the driver's seat, Michiko beside him, Jon and Ken in the back seat. But just after leaving the house, when they made the turn onto Sunset Boulevard, Ken reached over and grabbed a tuft of Jon's thick hair in his large hand. He pulled Jon's head up against his own and bit down into Jon's cheek.

"Ouch!" Jon screamed. "Cut it out, Ken!" His voice was changing, and the crack in his high-pitched shriek gave it a comic sound, like the cry of a stricken duck. But there was nothing funny about the blood oozing down Jon's chin from the teeth marks on his lacerated cheek. At once, a fight raged between the two boys in the back seat, arms and shoulders slamming against doors and windows, and Michiko became concerned that one of her sons might suffer a serious injury.

Jon gasped and shouted again, "Cut it out, Ken!" while Ken wailed, "K-i-i-i-e-e-h-e-e-h!" Al, crouched over the steering wheel, caught in the middle of traffic, could do nothing about the fight but throw nervous glances left and right. Nor was there anything Michiko could do to restrain her two boys physically; she was just too small for that.

When Al spotted the Gelson's Supermarket parking lot to his right, he pulled into it sharply. Jamming on the brakes, he jumped out of the car, opened the back door, and tried to wrest his sons apart. Ken's flailing hand grabbed Al's, and he dug his fingers into the soft palm.

"Stop it!" thundered Al. "Or I'll hit you, Ken."

105

As if Ken could understand his words. But it was enough to make Al the immediate target of Ken's fury. Ken grabbed what little thinning brown hair remained on Al's balding head and pulled it. Al was furious, but now realizing that his shouting would only make Ken pull all the more, lowered his voice to a whisper. "Leave go, Ken. Let go," Al pleaded, straining for breath, his bowed head turning red, the veins on his temples bulging.

As Ken was resisting Al's attempt to straighten his long fingers one by one in order to loosen his grip, Jon seized the opportunity by tumbling out of the car door on the other side. Michiko, too, got out of the car and tried to help Al. She reached back into the car for Ken's hand, but instead soon found herself unable to budge, her arm uselessly wedged between Ken and Al. She knew even if she had been able to grab hold of Ken's hand she still would have been no match for his strength, and that fact only heightened her feeling of utter helplessness.

Al gradually freed himself of Ken's grasp, and with his head still bent over as he gasped for breath, he said to Michiko and Jon, "Move away, both of you, so Ken can't see you. Let's just leave him alone in the car for the while." And then he quickly sprang back away from the opened car door, closing it behind him, and joined Michiko and Jon in squatting on the slightly raised curb, which bordered a thicket behind their parking space.

Behind them were a few newly planted Nandin trees dotted with red berries, their leaves rustling in the wind. But in the distance, beyond the building in front of them rose the sparsely wooded Santa Monica Mountains, dark clouds hanging so low over their peaks that it looked as though it might rain any moment. People pulling into the parking lot regarded the family on the curbstone curiously. Ken, on the other hand, could not see his family from where he was sitting. He was too busy striking himself on the head with his right hand and then banging his head against the car window.

"K-i-i-i-e-e-h-e-e-h!" His muffled monkeylike screech pierced the humid afternoon air. Michiko wondered how they could make the sixty-minute trip to BTC; it was barely five minutes since they had left their own house.

But within ten minutes, Ken suddenly seemed to notice that there was no one else in the car, and he stopped screaming and instead looked around. Michiko, relieved that he had become silent, prayed that he remain so; and crouching forward like a military scout on reconnaissance, returned to the car and nervously sidled up to the left rear window and peered in. Ken was continuing to study the scenery about him as if nothing had happened.

"Will you be a good boy now?" Michiko asked him.

Ken seemed surprised by her voice. His eyes turned toward her, rested upon Michiko for a second as if recognizing her, and then he slowly nodded. Michiko knew better than to trust his response completely; when he was in a good mood, he nodded no matter what the question, understanding more the fact that it was a question rather than

107

the question itself, because of the intonation in the speaker's voice. But Michiko decided that Ken had calmed down sufficiently for them to continue on, and cupping her hands together megaphone style, she called out to Al and Jon: "It's all right now!" And then, still very much like a military scout, she beckoned them forward with hand waves. Al rose from his curb perch; his shoulders brushed against a branch, and Michiko could see the red berries sway gently in response.

Now Al resumed command. Ken would sit in the front beside him, for the rest of the ride he said, and Michiko would feed him from the back seat, occupying and distracting Ken with food. For such emergencies, Michiko always brought along a brown paper bag full of the seedless Satsuma mandarin oranges Ken loved. And so, after the new seating arrangements were effected, the windows rolled down, and the car was back on the road again, she reached in and pulled out a mandarin, peeled away its pockmarked skin, quickly tore off a section, and dropped it into Ken's mouth. From her seat diagonally behind him she could see, in profile, Ken's cheek loosening as he swallowed the entire section without chewing it, some juice dribbling down his lips as he did so. And she relaxed.

But soon, Ken's long, delicate fingers spread out, reaching back over his shoulder for more. Michiko placed another section in his hand, taking care not to give it to him too quickly, trying to make the mandarin last as long as possible. By the time Ken finished his second mandarin, the car was filled with the sweet and tangy smell of mandarins mingled with the oily body odor of the teenage boys. But now Ken was bouncing playfully, a completely different child, and everyone felt enormous relief; the heavy burden they all shared had lifted.

When they arrived at BTC, they were greeted by the director of the facility, who looked as though she had just spent an hour painting her face. She wore so much mascara that it seemed to drip off her lashes; her eyelids were lined with blue, and her round face was painted in a kaleidoscope of colors. She reminded Michiko of a Kabuki actor still in stage makeup. Michiko had met the director before, but she could not help marveling anew at the garish appearance of this woman, who was also a mother. Michiko had some second thoughts about trusting her and actually leaving Ken in her charge. But then, she reassured herself, there were many women just like the director, who lacked taste in applying makeup.

The director introduced Michiko to her office assistants, who had her fill out forms and sign them as if they were receipts for merchandise. Al and Jon carried in the brand new Japanese rice cooker they had just bought at a Japanese market, and the twenty-five pound bag of the premium California rice that Ken liked so much. Michiko had also brought along *gyoza*, the Chinese dumplings that were Ken's favorite food. She hoped that these provisions would spare Ken the difficulty of having to adjust to new food and new surroundings at the same time, the familiar tastes making him feel more at home and less alone.

When they waved good-bye to Ken, who was draped over the couch of the spacious living room, he lifted his right hand, spread his fingers, and motioned to them as though he was beckoning them to come closer to him, rather than part from him, emitting his monkeylike screech all the while. And then as he watched them leave, he laughed and buried his face in the cushions of the couch. He did not have a tantrum; he did not even cry.

Al and Jon and Michiko stepped out into the darkening evening silently. Back on the San Diego Freeway, the three of them, who would normally chatter away, were still silent. But tears were rolling down their cheeks.

For the thirteen years Ken had been at home with them, it seemed to Michiko that she had not been able to do anything. There were mountains of work waiting to be done, dresses to be designed, sweaters to be knitted; her bedroom closet shelves were overflowing with yard cloth, handicraft material, woolen yarn. But contrary to her expectations, in the following three weeks she could not finish any work; in fact, she could not do any work at all.

Time passed slowly, as if a movie projector was suddenly operating at a reduced speed. Michiko would be sitting on a chair in the bedroom, just reading a newspaper, and would soon find herself in a daze, one moment staring at the tear Ken had clawed in the beige wallpaper in the shape of Hokkaido Island, and the next moment she could be sniffing the tattered fringe of the bedcover Ken constantly chewed upon, which was still suffused with his smell, wondering how she came to be doing that. And whenever she went for a walk, she reflexively looked about for Ken, automatically expecting to find him trailing behind her.

One day in the supermarket, when she found herself composing a mental list of all the purchases she ordinarily made when Ken was still at home—another container of milk, two more bottles of juice, additional vegetables, and of course, more oranges and apples and bananas and grapes, until her shopping cart, overladen with fruit, would be full to the top—a painful electrical charge surged through her from the tip of her nose to the bottom of her eyes, where tears uncontrollably welled up. Embarrassed, she pretended something was in her eye and dabbed away at it with her handkerchief and quickly removed her sunglasses from her shoulder bag and put them on. And at the check-out counter, seeing her diminished shopping load laid out before her, she consciously kept her upper lip stiff and somehow managed not to break down in tears again.

Michiko was reticent about mentioning her ongoing emotional struggles to Al. Her Japanese sensibility made it difficult for her to display her *yowami*—or vulnerability; she even wondered if for the Japanese *yowami* had the exact same meaning as emotion. And somehow it was as if, even though she had lived in America for almost two decades, she still could not escape her essentially

Japanese nature. In the same way, during those three weeks, she never once asked her husband how he was feeling. Instead, she often became annoyed with him when he did not talk, imagining that he felt relieved after placing Ken in BTC, while she was constantly thinking of Ken. What on earth is Ken doing at this very minute? Did he sleep well last night? Has he been going to the toilet without accidents? She even wondered if he might be carrying a grudge against his parents, bearing resentment against them. But then, she reminded herself, how did he know what it was to *feel* a grudge? In every waking moment, Ken's face, like that of a Japanese doll, never left her for even a single second.

One day when she went into their bedroom to get the newspaper, she happened to overhear Al talking on the phone to his friend Frank. "I have no excuse for not working because of Ken anymore, but I just can't work," he was saying. "I'm getting even less done now than I did while Ken was here. I just sit at my typewriter and stare at the wall like I'm in a daze, until I suddenly realize tears are rolling down my cheeks." Michiko was relieved, as she tiptoed out of the bedroom, to realize that Al was going through the same difficult time she was.

And perhaps so too had been Jon, young as he was. Michiko was especially concerned about him; with his piercing black almond eyes, he appeared more sensitive than most kids his age. Now, every day after coming home from school, he ran straight into his room and closed the door behind him. With Ken gone, no longer jumping up and down on the couch and the beds and running through the house making his loud peculiar sounds, the house was quiet. Either Jon was taking advantage of the calm in order to catch up on his schoolwork, or perhaps, in his own way, he was going through the same surprising mood change as his parents and was unable to put his heart into anything.

After all, if you suddenly visit a remote and tranquil mountain spot, far from the turmoil and tumult of a big city, Michiko thought, you will immediately find yourself in a strange and abstracted state of mind. Perhaps her family had found itself in such a state. Their nervous systems, accustomed to overstimulation for a prolonged period, were in a similar state of shock, not knowing exactly how to cope with the decreased work load.

But there could also be another reason for Jon's behavior, his retreat behind the closed door of his room, and Michiko flinched as she thought of it. Despite his size, Jon was still essentially a defenseless kid, powerless when it came to the real world, who might resent his dependence upon his parents. He had never said anything, but the day they placed Ken in the BTC residence he insisted on accompanying them there, maintaining that he wanted to see exactly what kind of place it was. Since then, Michiko felt guilty, the muscle in her armpit stiffening, whenever Jon came home from school and raced into his room, slamming the door behind him with an explosive bang. Perhaps he was worrying in his own way about his brother who had lived with him since the day of his birth? Although Ken did not talk, and had terrible tantrums, he was still his only blood brother in the world. Perhaps Jon identified with his brother, whom his parents had decided to separate from the family, and he was the one carrying a grudge.

Whatever their peculiar reasons, the members of this family, who had loved to laugh and joke loudly, had become silent. Without Ken around, there no longer were accusatory shouting matches about who should have been watching Ken when he urinated on the floor or threw his food from the table or chewed up another bedspread. It was as if their daily family life had become a shell, like a cast-off skin whose interior was empty.

Now, as the Honda approaches the top of the San Diego Freeway at Mulholland Drive, the roadway carved through the Santa Monica Mountains, steep cliffs rise on both sides, and Al, who has been sitting quietly at the wheel, suddenly flares up. "Why the hell do we have to pick Ken up so early? Five o'clock would have been fine. And I would have been able to get a little more work done."

Al's voice abruptly brings Michiko back to the reality of the present, and she turns and studies her husband, his head bent over the wheel, his face stiffened in irritation, only his eyes looking upward. It is the posture and expression he always assumes when he is angry—even when he is not driving. Michiko recalls the conversation she over-heard between Al and his friend: ". . . I just can't work. I'm getting even less done now than I did while Ken was here." And she cannot understand what on earth he is talking about. He is being ridiculous, she knows, but still she tries to answer him.

"Look, today is Friday, right? If we left at five o'clock, I figured the freeway would be really jammed with all those office-worker commuters leaving early for the weekend."

Al's head is still bent down over the wheel, his forehead creased in a wrinkle, his mouth closed in a straight line, his eyes looking upward. He quickly scans the freeway, his eyes darting from left to right. "There's not much traffic now."

"Of course," Michiko agrees. "That is why I picked this time. Because when we brought Ken to BTC it was a Wednesday afternoon at three-thirty, and already the freeway was so jammed with blue-collar workers that it took us over an hour and a half to get there. And we were so nervous all the while, because of the tantrum Ken had before we even got on the freeway. Don't you remember? Anyway, I figured if we picked him up at five o'clock, who knows when we would get home and how late it would be before I could prepare din-ner." Michiko speaks in a low voice, almost a na-sal one, looking down at her hands clasped in her lap.

"There's no reason for you to come with me. Who needs you? Just to pick up Ken."

Michiko thinks: Oh, there he goes again. Al never liked to drive her anywhere. And she could never quite understand the reason. If she were a child, it would be one thing, but she was not a child, she was an adult. And as an adult she had intelligence and possessed judgement. She could tell whether she was disturbing his work or not. He always made such a big deal about not disturbing his work, but when his lawyer came in from New York, Al chauffeured him around all over town, dropped him and his wife off at restaurants, and even drove them to the airport. And this was with Ken still at home, when all sorts of terrible problems could develop at any minute.

Michiko had drawn in her breath and said to Al: "Why don't you have a lawyer in Los Angeles? That would make sense. You certainly would not have to drive him to the airport. Just because your New York lawyer handles a lot of celebrities does not mean that you are going to become famous like any of them. Besides, a lawyer is supposed to earn his money by working for you, not the other way around. He should be entertaining you; you are his client, not vice versa."

As she spoke, Michiko became increasingly annoyed. The fact that her husband treated his lawyer with more deference than he did his wife really upset her. She elbowed him in the ribs and began to feel a little better. But then she remembered when they lived back east in the suburbs of New York. Leading into their town along Route 9 there was a steel suspension bridge, parallel to the railroad station, across a river that was no more than a swampland of reeds and cattails before it drained into the Hudson.

Whenever they returned to town, after a trip to the city or shopping in a nearby mall, as soon as Michiko heard the *tera-tera-tera* sounds of their car speeding over that bridge, she knew Al's face would stiffen and he would say, "I killed the day by driving you around. Why the hell don't you learn how to drive?"

Michiko heard it so often she thought, as the Japanese say, a callous would form in her ears. At the age of forty-five, she finally did learn how to drive and got her license. But she never would drive on the freeway. In her youth she had frightened easily and never quite developed athletically. And so certainly, now that she was older, it was too late for her to enter into any competition with a Mr. Kamikaze driving a Porsche or a Datsun 280Z or an Alfa Romeo. Indeed, if there were an Ogasawara School of driving, she would be its perfect exemplar; she could even be considered an Iemoto—or master—for when she drove on surface streets, such as the continually twisting and winding Sunset Boulevard, she grasped the gearshift with just three pronged fingers, just as one is supposed to hold the *chasen* tea whisk. When she had to change into the right lane, she turned her head back very slowly and gracefully; and when she changed to the left lane, she always bowed very politely toward any oncoming driver. Her driving speed was not much faster than an ordi-

117

nary walking pace, and often impatient teenagers driving behind her would become irritated, and when passing her they would blow sharply on their horns or give her the finger. But even then she would drive on, perfectly composed, unruffled, saying, "Be my guest. Go right ahead if you please." It was her extreme fear, of course, that was responsible for her air of utter calm and tranquility. But she also knew her serene driving style on the freeway could result in one of those chain-reaction accidents they showed on the evening news, involving several dozen cars.

"Again, you begin." Michiko says to her husband. She knows Al understands her better when she speaks in short sentences. And, of course, they have been through all this before. But still, out of the corner of her eye, she can see Al's face stiffen even more.

"Ken's teacher won't be there. She said that, didn't she? So you won't be able to see her. So there's just no point in your coming. And if I went by myself, then I could have left any time I wanted to."

"You were not going to do any work this afternoon anyway. You were going to have lunch with your friend Frank, which means you would have sat and talked and drank until three o'clock. And then you would have been in no condition to work anyway."

"Hey, keep your big mouth to yourself. Don't tell me how to use my time."

Al's tone upsets Michiko, but she does not want

her easily excitable husband to smash into the Mercedes running beside them or rear-end the Datsun in front of them, so she grips her teeth and does not talk back to him. "Ten more minutes of patience," she tells herself. Already, up ahead, she can see the bluish misty mountains of the Angelus Forest, and soon, the sign indicating that the Nordoff exit is just 1½ miles ahead. "Hold on for just a little longer,' Michiko tells herself, gritting her teeth all the harder.

After exiting the freeway they turn left and drive west, through huge water puddles formed by yesterday's rain, until they come to the corner of the Cal State Northridge campus, where a white cement sculpture stands. Michiko has now seen this sculpture several times, but still cannot quite decide whether it is a monogram composed of the college initials or an abstract work of art.

Al turns down the wide boulevard. Across from the campus is the row of residential tract houses, with similar terra-cotta tiled roofs, protruding double garages, and long driveways. Al pulls into one of them. On both sides of a red brick path leading to the entrance are azaleas, their pink flowers blossoming. Michiko runs to the door, turns the knob, and pushes it open.

Just off the foyer is the large living room, part of it converted for use as office space. There, a bespectacled young man is hunched over a desk covered with various forms of paperwork, pencils, and a telephone; beside the desk are rows of file cabinets. Sliding glass doors lead out to a large backyard covered with turf, the sun reflecting up from it, blinding Michiko within the otherwise darkened house.

In the backyard, three children are on swings, their jackets, red, yellow, and blue gyrating up and down, one after the other. A shadow on the couch to Michiko's left suddenly seems to come alive, screaming, "E-e-e-i-i-i." It is Ken, who looks as if he has been actually waiting there for a long time, as if he had been told that his parents were coming and understood that fact. Al, following behind Michiko, takes off his ocher-colored hat and places it on Ken's head. The bespectacled young man looks up at Ken's screams and, noticing Al and Michiko, rises. "Hello," he greets them and turns to Ken. "Your mommy and daddy are here." The expression on Ken's face seems to say, "Don't you think I know that already?"

Ken leaves his perch on the couch and comes over to Michiko and leans his head against hers. Michiko inspects the clothing he is wearing, blue corduroy pants, which she herself tailored for him, and a gray sweat shirt. Around the neck of the sweat shirt, three weeks ago brand new, is a big hole, the teeth marks indicating that Ken has chewed it through. Michiko puts her hand on Ken's shoulder, angling her arm slightly upward. Ken has grown a little taller. A dimple forms on Ken's right cheek as he barely brushes Michiko's cheek with his lips. Unlike his brother Jon, who plants big wet uncomfortable kisses upon her so often she takes it for granted, Ken never does anything more than that, the light touch of lips without power, his own unique form of kissing. He really wants to see me, Michiko thinks, and she is not sure whether she is happy or sad about it. But she is grateful for Ken's kisses. Since he does not possess speech, or any of the other usual means of communication, a kiss from Ken, even one so marginal, represents an extraordinary act of will, an enormous effort at emotional expression on his part.

Al and Michiko go to Ken's room to get his stuff. It is a simple bedroom, two beds, each against a wall between windows framed with reddish-brown velveteen curtains, a chest of drawers beneath them. In the closet at the right of the entrance, Ken's jacket dangles loosely amidst the clothing of his roommate, Casey. Michiko takes it down from the hanger. Then, from the drawers on the side of the chest near Ken's bed, she withdraws undershorts, T-shirts, sweat shirts, and pants, sufficient changes of clothing for Ken's weekend at home. Meanwhile, Al finds Ken's suitcase on the top shelf of the closet and brings it over to Michiko. She packs the suitcase neatly and latches it closed. Al picks up the suitcase with his right hand, and Michiko follows him out of the bedroom, back to the entrance foyer, where Al takes Ken by the left hand and leads him to the door. Until Michiko returns to the living room to tell the bespectacled aide that they will be bringing Ken back on Monday morning, neither she nor Al has said a word.

In the car, Ken, still wearing Al's ocher hat,

raises his voice in his form of song, repeating "Whoom. Whoom," and once the car begins to move, he somehow comes up with a rubber band, which he spins between his thumb and index finger as if he is making twine, both of his shoulders churning, all of his energy involved in the repetitive action. As he stares intently all the while at the rubber band, the same senseless sing-song sounds continue to emerge from his throat and through his nostrils, "Whoom. Whoom."

When they pull into their own driveway without having had a single incident occur, on either the Freeway or Sunset Boulevard, Michiko is relieved. And when she gets out of the car, the touch of chilly, wet sea air that greets her cheeks seems to refresh and revitalize her completely. The evening sun has already gone down beneath the ocean horizon. No matter how warm it is during the day in winter, in Southern California the temperature falls quickly in the evening. Michiko opens the car door, and Ken leaps out. She goes to the trunk and finds his red-and-blue quilted jacket, puts its on him, and pushes him gently, telling him to go play in the backyard. Unlike an ordinary child, Ken does not respond quickly to such a suggestion. Instead, he slowly weaves his way, taking his own sweet time, to the rattan basket-chair hanging in the carport.

A lemon tree in the corner of the yard has already begun to blossom with white flowers, tinted with purple. The lawn, rejuvenated by the long, continuous rains, gleams and sparkles as if emerald gems are scattered there in the gathering dusk. Michiko is enveloped by a great sense of peace. For three weeks, something has been missing from the landscape and now has been restored to its proper place. The squeaking sounds of the rattan basket-chair Ken is swinging from side to side on, *gi ko ki ki ki*, resonate through the quiet garden.

Al goes straight into the living room, whose large picture windows look out at the lawn in the front garden. He turns on the TV set, sits down on the couch, and stretches his feet out on the low coffee table before it, atop copies of *Time* magazine and the *Los Angeles Times* left open there, half read. On both sides of the couch are twin end tables, a porcelain lamp on each. Beside the TV set is the fireplace, protected by a glass screen, in which neither Al nor Michiko has ever lit a fire. They long ago decided to forsake the pleasures of such a romantic ambience; with Ken around it was just too dangerous.

In the kitchen, Michiko puts on her white apron and stirs the contents of the large silver pot on the stove before her. Since Ken's birth, she has never invited guests for a formal dinner, but now the sense of pleasurable anticipation with which she used to cook returns to her. She turns the burner on again. She removes lettuce and tomatoes and cucumbers and romaine and broccoli from the copper-tone refrigerator, so much taller than she. She arranges the vegetables on the counter. Then she unwraps the lettuce and romaine carefully and washes each leaf repeatedly before wiping it dry with a paper towel, tearing it into smaller pieces, and dropping it into a large glass salad bowl until it brims over. She peels the cucumbers and tomatoes and slices them thin, passes the broccoli through the boiling water, and adds them all to the salad. She picks up the bowl and brings it to the round white table in the dining area and places it in the center, thinking: Four is a very good number to cook for. It works out perfectly in terms of the size of the portions.

While Ken was gone, their life as a family seemed to have fallen apart completely, as if caring for Ken was all that bound them together. At mealtimes, Al and Jon, usually loquacious, no longer talked to each other or to Michiko. And without Ken's keening and crying and screeching, it was always eerily silent. They would each bring their plates to the table, hurriedly ingest their food, and then carry their dishes to the sink, rinse them under running water, and deposit them into the dishwasher. And that was it.

Perhaps that was the way an ordinary family usually lived, but Michiko was not used to it. She had felt a sudden lack in her life, a barren and unfilled inner void. What was missing, of course, was that joyful but also miserable tyranny of having to meet the neverending demands of a baby before even beginning to consider her own needs and dreams. For fifteen years, first with Jon and then Ken, she had had to function every day of her life with a baby in the house.

Sometimes when she considered her lot, so much of the joy of life squeezed away, so many of the basic human rights usurped, Michiko regarded people with normal families, who were unaware that there were such people as herself, with great bitterness. They could never understand that Ken's placement in a group residence such as BTC was no solution to her problem. Oh, that it were! But her problem would exist as long as she lived. Whether Ken was living with her or not, she would always feel an incompleteness at the center of her life. With Ken around, it was difficult to live fully; there was always something to do for him. But without him around it was impossible to feel anything but that part of her life was missing. She was forever thinking of all the little things she could—or should—be doing for Ken. There was no escape. She had a life sentence of gnawing, recurring, constant guilt.

When Ken was at home, cooking, for Michiko, was often a torturous chore. She assumed it was because everyone in the family had different food preferences, tastes, and dietary needs. Al had a high cholesterol level and therefore required a low-cholesterol regime, not unlike one found in the usual Japanese diet. But Jon would refuse to touch any Japanese cooking, insisting instead on the greasy American junk foods and fast foods his teen-age peers ate. Ken would eat anything except the junk foods and fast foods his brother favored and the *sashimi* that provided the best source of low cholesterol protein for his father. Just trying to satisfy this hodgepodge of conflicting tastes and needs, not to mention divergent schedules, could keep Michiko in the kitchen from morning to night.

Take dinner for example. Ken always ate first,

with Michiko hovering over him to supervise his manners and to anticipate his needs. Since he ate salad greens in the quantities that a horse devoured fodder, she had to ensure that enough mayonnaise was on the table. But not too much, because Ken, who would use a spoon or fork only when Michiko reminded him to do so, somehow always managed to dip his fingers right into the mayonnaise; and soon his hands, his face, his drinking glass, and his bowls and dishes were all the off-white yellowish color of mayonnaise. Michiko would give Ken a napkin with which to wipe himself. But he would disdainfully drop it fluttering to the floor while rice gathered on his lap or fell all around him.

Ken could eat prodigiously, second, third, fourth, and even fifth helpings—especially of rice—but eventually he would finish, rise, and try to make a hasty departure. Michiko would have to catch him with one hand as his lap emptied onto the floor, and with a cloth towel in the other hand, carefully wipe his mouth and hands, brushing away the bread crumbs and picking off the rice kernels still clinging to his shirt and pants. Michiko would then have to clean away his mess, tidy up the table, and then, at last she and Al and Jon could eat. At the same time she could not allow Ken to get too far out of sight—or sound range—because it was after eating that he was most likely to have a bowel movement or need to urinate. This part of the daily routine always left Michiko completely tired. And only during Ken's three-week absence did Michiko realize it was the effort involved in taking care of Ken alone that had so exhausted her, that Ken occupied most of her time and energy, that he consumed far more than one fourth of the oxygen in the family household.

The *oden* is done. Michiko decides that Ken, as usual, should eat first. She goes into the living room where she finds Ken sitting quietly next to his father. When she tells him to go wash his hands, he rises; he is definitely taller than she is now, but he is still a baby.

As she serves him his dinner, she does not feel herself tiring; her strength seems to have returned to her during his absence, and the process is cheerful, for Ken is quiet throughout the meal. She does not have to chase him back and forth between the kitchen and the living room, hawking her wares: "Here is your juice." "Do you want more potatoes?" "Drink your milk." Instead, Ken sits at the table patiently waiting for each new dish. When he finishes eating, Michiko wipes his hands and notices that the floor beneath him is practically clean; very little rice has dropped down upon it. She is so surprised she doubts her eyes, looks down to check again, and then is so delighted she wants to hug him.

As he leaves the table, Ken lightly touches his lips against Michiko's cheek in his form of kissing; and Al, entering the dining alcove, notices this. He looks at Michiko enviously and bends down and presses his face up against Ken's. "Give me a kiss, too." Ken ignores his cheek and darts off into the living room. Al's eyes follow Ken's leaping back. "He won't kiss me," he says sadly.

Michiko is happy. Unlike her husband, kissing does not mean very much to her. Since she is Japanese, she was not brought up with the custom— especially, the custom of indiscriminate kissing. Americans are forever kissing. They kiss when they wake up and they kiss when they go to sleep. They kiss each other when they arrive at a party, even though they may detest each other, and then kiss each other again before leaving, even though they may now truly hate each other. And it seems if they are not kissed, they feel rejected. But no matter how long Michiko has lived in the West, she still cannot really understand the psychology involved in being happy when you are kissed and disappointed when you are not kissed, especially if you do not usually care a whit about the person who is kissing you. Perhaps it is the habit of childhood, and Al is just being childish in showing his disappointment. He should know that Ken, being as he is, has no intention of demonstrating any preference.

"Al, do you want some *sashimi*?" she asks her husband, who is just standing there absentmindedly as she collects Ken's plates and silverware.

Her words seem to bring Al back to himself. He stares at her through his eyeglasses and answers drily, "Sure."

"Well, it is in the refrigerator."

While Michiko goes to the sink to rinse Ken's dishes before placing them in the dishwasher, Al opens the refrigerator and removes the small packet of *sashimi*. It is in pink wrapping paper, covered with a layer of plastic. Al tears off the vinyl and barks, "Who wrapped this?"

128

Michiko does not like his tone. She slams the dishwasher door shut and turns around to face him. Al is glaring at her, his eyes ready to pop out of their sockets. "I did," she says defiantly. "I wrapped it. Who else?"

"How many times have I told you that if you wrap something you're putting in the refrigerator with vinyl you're insulating it. Which means you're keeping the heat in. Which means it will spoil."

Michiko cannot help but raise her voice. "It has no heat to begin with. The *maguro* was cold and fresh when the Japanese fish man left his house yesterday morning. The *maguro* was still cold and fresh when I bought it on his refrigerated truck, parked in our driveway yesterday afternoon. It is now winter, not summer, and it was raining when I brought it into the house. There was no chance for any heat to get into the *maguro* between his truck and this kitchen. And after taking all of that into consideration, I decided to wrap it in plastic. So is what I did so terrible?"

But Al is barely listening to her. His forehead is already creased in anger. "Yes, it's terrible. Because it's already spoiled; it's all rotten, that's why. Why can't you listen to me? How many times do I have to tell you something?"

"It is not spoiled. It is not rotten," Michiko punches out each word clearly. "It is cold, and it is fresh."

Al's face flushes, the blue veins in his temples throb conspicuously, and his voice seems to hit the ceiling and reverberate throughout the room. "And I tell you it's rotten. Because you don't know how to use a refrigerator. You don't wrap meat or fish in plastic before placing it in the refrigerator."

There is no reason for Al to get so angry and upset. Michiko cannot understand if her husband is right or wrong, scientifically. When they were first married, she was certainly no expert on American refrigeration, but she still is not so sure Al is one either. After all, when she buys fish or meat in an American supermarket, it always comes wrapped in plastic. He is in a bad mood. Ken's not kissing him did not help matters, so perhaps he is just looking for an excuse to get angry.

But if that is the case, she will not just back off timidly. Her credo, throughout her life, has always been, "Never be defeated by the irrational." That was why she left Japan. That was her way of thinking. Maybe at times she is too quick to argue with Al instead of simply agreeing and saying, "Oh, yes, certainly," and bowing politely and obediently. But she would hate herself if she did that. She could have stayed in Japan to act like that. So even though Japan was defeated by America a long time ago, automatically just saying "Yes" to an American still goes against her grain. She was that way when she came to America twenty years ago, and she has not changed, not even when it comes to domestic squabbles. Sometimes she feels petty in forcing Al to uphold America's political positions, to defend America's failure to solve its social problems. It even seems as if she is trying to achieve, in some measure, revenge in America for defeats in Tokyo. But that is not so this time. Al is simply being irrational, and she will not violate her credo.

She lifts her eyes, and her pretty eyebrows, and stares at her husband's auburn eyes behind his glasses. "Open the *sashimi*. Go ahead. See if it is spoiled. If it is spoiled, you can be angry with me. But do not get angry with me before you know whether it is spoiled or not. Until then, you have no right to shout at me!" she herself shouts.

Still catching her breath, Michiko goes to the doorway and looks into living room to check on Ken. She can never allow herself to forget about him for a single second—even in the middle of an argument; after all, he might have to go to the bathroom. But Ken is sitting peacefully on the beige couch behind the coffee table, and he seems to be watching television, the seven o'clock network news, his eyebrows gently arced, just like Michiko's. Never mind that he probably does not understand a word of it. Michiko cannot recall Ken ever having just quietly watched television before, so that in itself represents great progress; she is pleased that he is behaving so well.

In the kitchen, Al still has not unwrapped the fish. "Open the package quickly," she tells him. "Before it spoils even more."

Al slowly removes the plastic and pulls back the pink paper. Beneath it, another thin white paper is wrapped around the raw tuna fish. Al slowly peels that paper back, and there is blood scattered on it along with the pinkish-red tuna. It is obviously still fresh, but Michiko makes a point of bending over and sniffing it. The overhead fluorescent light, in its reverse Go board plastic hood, sounds like water slowly running out of a faucet. Dry hot air flows out of the heating vent in the corner, and Michiko feels herself perspiring slightly. What does Al know about fresh fish? Or his ancestors for that matter? They all came from deep within Russia— far from sources of fresh fish. No wonder so many of them have a history of thyroid problems.

Her finger is still pointed downward at the *maguro*. Like a lawyer about to trip up a witness in a courtroom cross examination, she looks up at him. "Is this spoiled? Do you call this spoiled?" she demands. "You always judge something before you look at it. It is a terrible habit you have, all through our marriage. Do you remember, after we were married just a couple of weeks, when I cooked roast beef? You stamped your feet and yelled and screamed how it was overcooked and too well done? I have never forgotten it. I could barely speak English at the time. I was so enraged my blood was boiling. But I could not shout back at you because I did not have the English words with which to do so. Instead, all I could do was say, 'Please cut it and see.' And you sliced it and it was just right, the way you liked it, medium rare.

"But that was not the end of it for me. I stayed up all night crying to myself: 'Why have I married such a person?' And the next day I said to you very slowly, 'Please do not prejudge things.' I had composed that sentence carefully during the night. It was all I could say, and I kept repeating it over and over again, which only infuriated you more and more. And again we had a fight, a big fight. You even lost your temper and threw an ashtray at me. And I became so frightened I took down my suitcase and began to pack. I decided I would go back to Japan immediately, because I refused to live with a man who could be violent. I packed all my things and asked you to please call a taxi. We were living in Brooklyn Heights at the time, not far from the waterfront, and many Japanese cargo ships docked there, so it would be easy to return to Japan that way. Do you remember?

"This all happened twenty years ago, but still you have not changed. How many times have we repeated this same scene during these twenty years? And how many times have I reminded you of it? When I married you I thought I could change you. But I guess the human brain can never change." And as she sighs deeply, her shoulders drooping, she wonders what Al's behavior and her own outburst have to do with Ken's homecoming.

Al does not say anything. Only the whirring running-water sound of the fluorescent lighting fixture breaks the silence. For a moment, Michiko fears that he might be so stubborn as to insist that what obviously is not spoiled is spoiled. But when Al finally does speak, he merely restates the argument they had earlier in the day. "I was annoyed because you made me waste half a day. If you had not insisted on coming along, I could have picked Ken up at six."

"You never give up," Michiko says, "do you?

You have to keep bringing up the fact that I went with you this afternoon."

"That's because there was no reason for you to come with me."

"I am a parent. I am Ken's mother. I was anxious to see his face as soon as possible. I also wanted to see the room he was living in and the faces of the people who work there. I was simply curious."

At the word "curious," Al stops frowning. "It's a different story if you were curious."

"You are a writer and after twenty years of living with me you do not know that I am a curious person. Especially when it comes to matters involving my own son when he is living outside of my house. What kind of mother would I be if I was not curious?"

They finally sit down to dinner, calling Jon in from his room. When he comes to the table and sees the *oden*, Jon makes a sour face; Michiko has not prepared any special American dish for him. Al dips a piece of his *sashimi* into a mixture of *wasabi* and soy sauce on a small white saucer and smiles over to Jon, "Want to go to a movie after dinner?"

What is Al up to? It seems to Michiko as if he has decided not to give up completely, not to concede that she has been right all day long, about both the best time to pick up Ken and the way in which to wrap raw fish. Now he is evidently trying to involve Jon on his side with a little bribery. Because the two of them never go to the same movie. They could never enjoy it. Their tastes differ too much. Jon always wants to see pictures about space and war, two subjects in which she knows Al has absolutely no interest.

Al notices the puzzled expression on her face as she looks from one to the other, and he smiles. "I figure it's a good opportunity for Jon and me to go somewhere together. Since Ken is home, you won't have to be alone in the house," he says. "You know how you're afraid to be alone in the house at night."

Isn't my husband sneaky, Michiko thinks, throwing back my own words at me? A few weeks ago, she had told them both that when Ken was at home she was less afraid to be left alone in the house at night. That was because not a day passed without reports in the newspaper and on television of numerous murders and rapes and countless thefts and burglaries. Most recently it was the Hillside Strangler, littering the mountains with the corpses of his young female victims. They had finally caught him. But in America, because of the peculiar nature of the society, another serial killer always seems to come along. They have no gun control, but are permissive when it comes to the buying and selling of drugs. As a result, too many people with damaged brains, unable to distinguish between good and evil, are walking the streets armed with dangerous weapons.

Of course, it could be argued that even both Al and Jon staying at home could not fend off an armed intruder. But they still would put up a stronger fight than she alone. Besides it seems that women who are alone are always the prime targets of these serial killers. That was why she said what she did.

"Ken was some *yojinbo!*" Al had said.

"What's a *yojinbo?*" Jon asked.

"A bodyguard," Al said, and they both laughed.

"At least Ken's big, and the intruder does not know about his condition," she had said at the time.

But now, sitting about the same table, she tells her husband and son, "I am amazed. And I am disappointed in both of you. Why do you think we brought Ken home? So he could be with us. Can't you just give him two days of your time?"

"You mean we're supposed to follow Ken around all weekend? If he goes to the toilet, all three of us have to go to the toilet, too? If he takes a bath, the three of us have to wash him?" Al has been addressing Michiko but looking at Jon. Now he turns to her. "You have no right to tell us what to do or how to behave, Michi. It's better for Ken if we all just act normally and that he find this house in its natural state. For example, I'm still going to go to my office to work tomorrow, and I think it's perfectly all right for Jon to go play with his friends as usual."

"But things are different now," says Michiko. "Ken has not been here all week long. We do not have the excuse that he has been taking up all our time during the week, so that we have to work on weekends. I know I am ready to devote myself to Ken completely for the next two days. And you should be, too."

"Don't tell me what to do," Al shouts at her. "Don't start ordering me around in a loud voice!" When he closes his mouth, the vein in his temple starts twitching.

Michiko's voice tops his. "You are the one who raised his voice first!"

Al's voice is suddenly unnaturally soft. "No. You raised your voice first."

Michiko's answer is almost a whisper. "No, it was you. But if you want to insist it was me, fine, okay. But if I raised my voice, it is only because when I talk to you, you do not listen. I have to use a loud voice just to get your attention. But I am not shouting. I am just trying to get through your blocked ears and get you to listen."

"Maybe I don't listen because I don't want to listen."

"Exactly. When we were first married I thought you were deaf, but I was not sure. Maybe it was just my English you could not understand? But then I soon realized that I had to shout in order to get your attention. Otherwise, nothing would ever get done."

Michiko peeks into the living room where Ken is still quietly watching the television set beside the fireplace. The reflection of his figure, in the bright light of the white porcelain lamp on the end table, in the glass screen of the fireplace is like a Bonnard painting. The news is over and now the shrill voice of a game show host greets a cheering audience, whistling in excitement. Ken is still lying on the couch, his head cupped in his right hand, a detached expression beneath his widely separated eyebrows, like a sleeping, or reclining, Indian Bud-

137

dha. (His frame is too big and he is too long-limbed to be a Japanese Buddha.) His hair has grown so long in the past few weeks that he does not quite look like himself. But also, happily, he is not acting his usual self, jumping up and down like a mechanical doll, and Michiko is pleased that he is so well behaved. Better behaved than his parents, in fact. What kind of welcome are we giving him? What kind of parents are we? Shouting at each other his very first evening home. She is ashamed of her own conduct, but at the same time she will not back off and kowtow to her husband. Not now. Not ever. Especially when he is wrong, especially when he starts it.

She returns to the dining alcove, puts her fist around a chopstick, and tattoos the table with it. "I do not shout all the time," she says, enraged. "You are the one who starts it, and I just answer back your loud voice with my louder voice; your harsh words with my harsher words. But you are the one who always starts it, and if we had a tape recorder I could easily prove it." She hears her own voice echoing throughout the house; it even fills her own head painfully; and she feels, most acutely, sorrow for Ken. He returns home after his first absence, his first trip away from home, and if he could talk he would probably be saying, "I do not like it here. I do not like the noise. I want to go back to BTC."

Jon, who has barely touched his food, lays down his fork and leaves the dining alcove, weaving his way between his quarreling parents and then through the living room back to his own room.

The notion of anyone's going to a movie seems to depart with him. Michiko and Al eat on silently, mechanically, the blood in their heads rather than in their stomachs as they stare angrily at each other.

Michiko wants to end hostilities, to have peace again. If she changes the subject maybe that will help change the mood. "After I clear the table," she says, "I want to cut Ken's hair. It has grown so long it almost covers his eyes. Will you help me?"

"Ah—" Al answers with a vague shrug, stands up, pushes his chair in, and goes off through the living room toward the bedroom.

Michiko sponges the table clean, sadly wiping away Ken's mayonnaise finger painting. She gathers the dishes, piles them in the sink, and washes her hands. Then she goes into the living room and, bending her hand back toward herself to make the American hand signal, says, "Come here." The reclining Buddha springs to his feet and comes leaping into the dining alcove.

Michiko calls out, "Al," as she sits Ken down at the table again and tells him to clasp his hands together on the white tabletop. He does so, assuming the position of a penitent in prayer. This is the position Ken has been taught at BTC, the theory being that with his hands engaging each other he will not grab and clutch at people. Michiko rewards him with verbal praise, "Good sitting, Ken," she says, and goes to the refrigerator to get a cluster of grapes and a plastic spray bottle full of ice water. BTC has instructed her to use the ice water as a punishment for Ken when he refuses to follow instructions or misbehaves badly. A spray of it on the tender skin of the cheek is a stingingly painful but harmless punishment.

Al sullenly returns to the dining alcove and stands behind Ken with the bunch of grapes in his hands. From the second drawer on the right-hand side of the L-leg counter, Michiko extracts a pair of five-inch scissors and begins to cut the long hair growing down Ken's neck. Straining her fingers, she squeezes the scissors as hard as she can because Ken's hair is even thicker than her own coarse Japanese hair. Again and again, she cuts away a tuft, and Ken seems to be weathering what is usually an ordeal for him; after each cutting, Al rewards him by popping a grape into his mouth and saying, "Good boy, Ken."

Now Michiko circles around Ken to see where she should cut next, and Ken moves his head slightly as his eyes follow her, and he unclasps his fingers. "Good sitting," Michiko says firmly and begins to snip away at the hair growing down over his forehead. But Al, who is about to pop a grape into Ken's mouth, suddenly suspends his hand in midair and shouts, "What the hell are you saying?"

A shocked Michiko lowers her head and says to herself, "Oh no, here he goes again!" It seems just about anything will set Al off tonight. She casts an upward glance at him and turns to Ken, who is still awaiting his expected reward for allowing another tuft of his hair to be cut—a grape; his eyes are glued to the cluster in Al's hand. But Al is too

excited to notice Ken or the wrinkle forming between his eyes, and Al's hand, holding the grapes,
moves in all directions as he shouts, "I'm in charge
of Ken. I'm giving him the commands and the
rewards. You shouldn't tell him anything."

Ken's eyes follow the movement of the grapes in
Al's hands, up and down and from side to side.
Michiko just stands there, still in shock, her hands
against her hips, the blades of the scissors in her
right hand spread open. In a typical American
domestic dispute, at this point, the scissors might
be used as a bloody weapon. But fortunately
Michiko can remain calm. Only in terms of her
hands, however, not in terms of her mouth. "I am
the one who is cutting his hair. What am I supposed to do? I cannot cut his hair if he is moving
around. So before cutting it I said 'good sitting,' to
make him sit still. What is wrong with that?"

"I'll tell you what's wrong," Al screams. "You
know that two people cannot control him at once.
Only one. Ken cannot handle orders coming from
two different people."

"You did not tell me you would control him."

"I'm the person giving him the reward. That
mean's I'm the person who is controlling him. It's
so obvious. How stupid can you be?"

"You have such bad timing that any order you
give him is ineffective. But if you are so deter-
mined to control him, you should also cut his hair.
Here." She pushes the scissors toward Al. "Cut
Ken's hair yourself. You've never done it."

Instead of taking the scissors, Al holds up his

hand and falls back a step. "You don't understand," he says. "When you say, 'good sitting,' that
sounds to Ken as if you're praising him for sitting
exactly the way he is at the moment. What you
mean to say is, 'Do good sitting.' Otherwise, you're
only confusing him."

Michiko pushes the scissors further toward Al's
stomach. There is a strange gleam in the corners
of her eyes. Al just stands there, clutching the
grapes to his chest. The scissors are like two dag-
gers about to leave Michiko's hand. But Al is still
unwilling to admit that he does not know how to
cut Ken's hair. Michiko pulls back the scissors and
shakes her head. "English is not my mother tongue,
you know. I did not know there was that subtle
difference in meaning. You should have told me
about it before, or simply explained it to me just
now, quietly, and I could have understood it. Instead, at the worst possible moment, the most
dangerous time, you just exploded. It was the wrong
time. You have never cut his hair, and you had no
idea of the problem I was having with Ken's moving around."

Ken spreads his long white fingers apart, waves
his hands in the air and shouts, "Wooh! Wooh!"
His hands are so huge that one of them can cover
Michiko's head completely.

Al commands in a stern voice, "Clasp your hands
in front of you, Ken." In reply, Ken's huge hand
swoops down onto Al's hand holding the grapes
and scratches it. A red line of blood is soon stream-
ing down the back of Al's hand. Al looks down at

it. The scowl of anger is on his face again, and he raises his left hand and slaps Ken across the face. Michiko fears that Ken will now become so upset that he will really go off on a rampage. She is so furious with her short-tempered husband that big teardrops form in her eyes and her throat begins to burn. Yet, strangely, Ken remains calm.

But Michiko is reluctant to proceed any further. "That's it," she tells her husband. "I cannot cut his hair anymore. It is too dangerous to go on. You should never have slapped him." Her body stiffens. Her voice is hoarse, and she can taste the salt in her tears.

Ken, sensing something unusual is going on, swings his head from side to side restlessly. But Al will not give up, he just cannot stop. "It's so uneven here." He points to Ken's forehead. "The left and right sides have different lengths."

Michiko is beside herself. "I told you, I am not cutting his hair anymore. If you want his hair cut straight, do it yourself. Poor Ken! He finally comes home and look at the way you treat him. By blowing your top. You are the one who is out of control." Angrily, she slams the scissors onto the table, not caring in the least what happens next.

But what happens next is this: Ken, who has been sitting there babbling and singing while rotating his head, scoots down from his chair and picks up the scissors. He runs to the L-leg counter, opens the second drawer on the right-hand side, places the scissors there, and closes the drawer. Then he swoops into the living room, his shoulders shaking, his head bent forward, flops down on the couch sideways, and rests his head in his hand, his arm bent at the elbow, resuming his position as a recumbent Buddha.

Al and Michiko are both amazed that Ken knows exactly where the scissors go. But they register no surprise in the expressions on their faces, suppressing any sign of their astonishment as if by some tacit understanding.

Michiko tries to fathom the reasons behind Al's sudden bursts of temper. One possible explanation could be the faulty diet of his ancestors, generation after generation rarely eating vegetables and subsisting solely on a diet of greasy meat. But there is also a simpler explanation: the fact that he is a writer, and in every society writers are not normal. In any case, she wonders, how could I have lived with him and such craziness for the past twenty years? Have I been ignoring half of his personality? Do people always try to overlook those qualities they do not know how to deal with?

"You were being difficult," Al is saying. "That's why I exploded."

"You were the one who was being difficult. I was not being difficult. It was you. And now you are trying to blame me for your fault. You always try to turn things around. You are really good at doing that. And if you are like this now, I can just imagine what you are going to be like when you get old, when every personality flaw magnifies in intensity. You will really be disgusting. It makes me worry about my future, because then I just will not have the patience to put up with a person like

144

you. I also have to worry about the future of your progeny. Ken, with all of his other problems, also has a terrible temper. And Jon, too, just like you, loses his temper too easily. And his school record is poor, just like yours was. And then there is your sister, unmarried and depressed, and who knows what problems she will cause? I am sick of taking care of your lousy genes. I did not come to America to take care of crazy people. I came here to search for my own freedom and independence. I am going back to Japan."

Michiko looks out the kitchen window at the already darkened ocean, but she cannot find a single light gleaming in the distance in any direction. "With Ken at BTC and coming home just for weekends, you and Jon can manage without me." The tearful whine of her own words only increases her distress, and she knows that Al is thinking, "There she goes again." But at the same time, she also knows he is scared out of his wits, because he is aware that he has a quick temper and that it is his responsibility to control it no matter what the provocation. Once, a long time ago, she had tried to teach him Zen meditation. But he could not even sit still for two minutes of it.

"You're the one who's been so nervous and anxious all day," Al insists.

"I was joyous. I would be seeing Ken today. My mood was up, my spirits soaring to the sky. But since the freeway you have just been one big pain after another. You should realize that. Blame yourself. If you admit just this once that you started it, then I will be willing to forget about it."

"Okay, I'll admit it just this once," Al says in slow, measured tones. "Maybe I was wrong and I did start it. I do have a short fuse, and I'm responsible for its getting lit. But you also have to admit that you poured a little oil on the fire, too." He stares into Michiko's wet eyes. But Michiko can only sob, ashamed of her own stubbornness. She picks up one of the brown paper napkins still on the table and blows her nose into it.

But even Michiko has to admit to herself in all honesty that she had anticipated Ken's return home with mixed feelings. Although she looked forward to seeing him, wondering about how he might have changed, she also felt great pangs of guilt in having ignored him. So there was much she wanted to do for him to make up for it. But at the same time, she was also afraid that she had become too accustomed to her newfound leisure to be able to handle Ken at all. Al, too, must have had similar fears and expectations. But while Al, as an American, showed his emotional confusion in his behavior, she, as a Japanese, could not express her feelings with such openness. And even when Al revealed his vulnerability, she was just too single-minded to calm him down reassuringly. But that was not completely her fault either. Taking care of the child-giant, Ken, demanded all the resources of her tiny body; she just did not have the energy to deal with any distractions.

On Monday morning, after driving Ken back to the BTC residence, Michiko and Al can finally relax. Their sense of relaxation is not like that of other people, who do not have problems such as theirs; in fact, it is not even like any sense of relaxation they ever had before placing Ken in BTC. It is as if all of a sudden the very core, the hard center of their emotional lives, has been blown away, and now they can feel only the utter quietude that comes after a storm is over.

The white mini-blinds on the windows in the dining room are open. A soft light flows in through the horizontal slats. The Boston fern suspended from the ceiling looks like delicate green lace woven upside down. After lunch, Michiko brews *hojicha* and pours it in two *kutani* tea cups. She places one in front of Al and the other before herself. This newfound serenity, she thinks, could even last the week.

But the jangle of the telephone on the counter shatters the silence. Al hurries to the phone, his teacup in hand, and answers it. "Hello," he says, still sipping his tea. "Frank, how are you?" Frank is a British-born writer friend who lives in their neighborhood.

"I'm fine." Michiko can overhear Frank's crisp, accented nasal voice. "But how was your weekend with Ken?"

"Ah Frank, what can I say," Al sighs. "Ken was terrific, easy to handle, and he behaved very well. The problem was us, Michi and me. We were constantly fighting over nothing. Even before he set foot in the house. I felt sorry for Ken."

"It's always that way, isn't it?" Frank's cackling filled the room. "It's the same at our house. Whenever we're expecting guests, especially from afar,

Mary and I both become agitated and are soon at each other. About who'll do this, and who'll do that, and who'll go pick them up. And we both make a big deal out of the most trivial detail, something neither of us would normally ever notice, and then we blame each other for forgetting to take care of it. It's only natural. It always happens. So just think of Ken as a guest or a visitor, and you and Michi need not get so pissed off at each other."

As she hears Frank's words, Michiko turns to Al and seeks out his eyes. He is staring back at her with eyes as moist as her own.

"Ken has become a guest," Michiko tells herself, and holding the warm teacup with both hands, she peers out the window at the ocean in the early afternoon light—and then far beyond it.